MEMORIES THAT COST A LIFETIME: The Immortal War Collection

Stories by:

XIRCON

James Glass

Suzi M

Ann Ominous

Smiling Goth Productions

www.SmilingGoth.com

ISBN-13: 978-0-615-26001-3

First edition paperback, October 2008.

Author contact suzi@smilinggoth.com

Visit The Hanging Cages in Second Life:
http://slurl.com/secondlife/Agravain/140/239/78

Check SmilingGoth.com for updates, additions, book release parties and events.

Foreword:

It's been a long crazy ride from the early days of SmilingGoth.com from the official launch in October of 1998. We've had some great times, and made some great friends along the way.

The stories contained in these pages are a collection from 1994 shorts to snippets featured at one time on the website, to fragments that never saw the light of day.

Each story deals with an event occurring within the 20 year time-span between the novels LAMIA and THE TOWER.

Enjoy.

~ Suzi

IN THE HANGING CAGES

By

XIRCON

The music pulsed and swirled, too loud and likely to draw attention from the cops, but tonight Paul—Poe to those who knew him in the business—didn't give a good goddam about the authorities. He was in his element, he was making money hand over fist and it was all profit, no expenses. He glanced up at the women in the hanging go-go cages as they writhed against duct tape and handcuffs. All profit....

"How much for the one on the left?"

Poe turned to see that the speaker/shouter was a middle-aged man with streaks of silver in his dark brown hair. Severe brown eyes stared at Poe and he shifted uncomfortably. The one thing he hated about his business was the clients.

"Three thousand," he shouted in answer.

The man pulled a wad of cash from his black overcoat and sorted the American dollars from the various European currencies. He handed Poe three thousand in smaller bills and added a hundred.

"For your troubles," the man told him and Poe smiled.

Getting what this guy wanted had been easier than anyone would have thought. He nodded across the dancefloor to his DJ/assistant and motioned to the left-hand cage. Carlos—a.k.a. The Phreak—nodded and moved from the soundbooth to a small control board. They could work the lights and any additional special effects from the board, including raising and lowering the go-go cages.

The anonymous buyer next to Poe stared hungrily at the cage as it and its occupant were lowered to the floor. The naked young blond woman inside the cage seemed to dance to the music, but Poe knew better. His go-go dancers never danced. He unlocked the handcuffs on the woman's bleeding wrists and relocked them behind her back. He turned back to the man with the severe brown eyes.

"She's all yours."

"Thank you!" The man shouted over the music and waved to Poe as he placed his coat over the woman's trembling shoulders. Poe wondered if the man would take off the duct tape covering her eyes and mouth before leaving the club. Not that it mattered. They never lived long enough to be witnesses.

The crowd grew around midnight, as it always did, and became gradually larger until around the wee hours before sunrise. Technically, according to New York law, Poe was supposed to be closed long before that, but then again, he wasn't really supposed to be open at all. His club had been shut down long ago. Now he claimed it as living quarters and paid off any cops that needed to be convinced there was no club goings-on in there.

Poe grinned as he pocketed the money he'd made, his thin pinched features barely brought to amusement by the expression. He had gained the name Poe in high school, when a couple of the more popular kids had actually paid attention in English class one day and decided that Paul Ellison was the modern-day reincarnation of Edgar Allen Poe. The fact that Paul's middle name was Orson (his parents had both been sadistic fanatics of Orson Welles) had only sealed his fate. Paul Orson Ellison had been known from then on as P.O.E. He'd just dropped the punctuation between the letters eventually to be Poe. Very few people knew his real name, and fewer still knew how he'd come to be known as Poe.

He sold four women and two men that night,

totaling over twenty-two thousand dollars. He charged depending on "difficulty of acquisition", it sounded so much more professional than "kidnapping" or "abducting". The harder it was to "acquire" a person, the more his buyer had to pay. As a general rule Poe charged more for the men. They were a pain in the ass to get, and a bigger pain to keep. And they just didn't have the dramatic flare in the cages that the women had. Poe only stocked the men by appointment usually. It was just easier. He made his way through the crowd of milling, mostly black-clad clientele to the soundbooth. It was a relief to get out of the loudness for a few minutes.

"How much you pull tonight?"

"Twenty-two. And that's not counting door cover."

The Phreak's expectant grin turned into a laugh. "You the bomb, man."

"Word," Poe tried, but they both knew he was too white to be accepted in an inner city crowd.

"Forget it, whitey. Maybe next lifetime

you'll be born with more soul."

Poe laughed and handed half of the night's earnings to his partner in crime, no pun intended.

"I'll be back with the door prizes after we close, 'kay?"

"Fine by me."

They kissed briefly and Poe left the booth, feeling his lover's stare on him all the way through the crowd. They'd been together since college, and had finally found a spot for themselves in the underground club scene. Good thing, too, since most of their clients slept underground.

And now, here they were, in The Hanging Cages, *their* club. The crowd that came through the door was mostly word-of-mouth and they didn't care about a couple of *gay* men with a club, they cared about the merchandise. Satisfaction all but guaranteed. All of his customers eventually came back, and none asked any questions.

A light touch to his shoulder sent a chill up his spine and charged the fillings in his teeth. He turned to see blackness and his heart froze for a moment before he realized he was looking at someone's chest. His eyes wandered up the massive form to be captured by a familiar silver stare.

"I need one of your dancers for my master," the gravelly voice informed him.

Poe grimaced and looked away. This guy was a regular customer. Apparently there were two of his kind, but the other one was a mess that actually made this guy look good… and if Poe didn't know better, he'd have sworn this guy's buddy had wings tucked under the huge overcoat.

"Look, Mr.…."

"Nivek."

"Mr. Nivek

"No, just Nivek. That is my name, as yours is Paul Ellison."

He stared up at the man, his face twisting unconsciously. For the first time he noticed the sharp, almost jagged features of his client, and the longish spiky jet-black hair. This Nivek guy looked like death warmed over. He wondered how many other clients knew his real name.

"OK, Nivek, how'd you find out my name."

It was more a demand than a question and Nivek's large eyes seemed to glitter and glow in the darkness as he stared down at Poe. The creature shrugged and a smile touched the corners of his lips.

"I can see it in your mind," he replied, "as I am sure many others here can do as well. You would be advised to guard your thoughts from your 'clients'. They are not all willing to pay such high prices for their survival."

"So why are you so willing to pay my prices?"

Again Nivek shrugged. "I have no choice in the matter. My master needs to survive."

"Alright, so why not tell your master to go to hell and get his own meals?" Poe hated to admit it, but this freak of nature was giving him some wonderful conversation.

"If he were free to hunt and kill for himself, be assured that he would. It is not for love of him that I supply him with food, it is for his… wife." Nivek closed his eyes as if he were in pain at the mere mention of the last word. Then it dawned on Poe exactly what was going on.

"You're in love with her, aren't you? In fact, judging by your expression, I'd say the only reason you don't kill your master is because you love his wife. Am I right?"

Nivek nodded and sighed. On a whim, Poe took the creature by one of his massive arms and led him up to his own personal living space.

"As weird as it sounds, I feel like we're friends, and you, Nivek, need a cup of coffee and some time to relax." Poe pointed to a chair, "Have a seat and make yourself comfortable. I'll get the coffee."

"What about your other customers?"

Poe shrugged and waved a hand. "Carlos can take care of it for a little while. Besides, since we opened, you and your weird buddy have been our best clients."

Nivek stared at him blankly for a few moments while he folded his overcoat over the arm of a chair, then brightened. "You are referring to Eldritch."

Poe shrugged as he scooped instant coffee into two mugs. "I guess so. I gotta ask just one question, though. Is it my imagination, or does uh… Eldritch?"

Nivek nodded.

"Yeah, does he have wings?"

The faint hint of humor danced into a smile on Nivek's face and Poe's jaw fell open in shock. A set of perfectly carnivorous teeth smiled over at him from Nivek's mouth, then were quickly concealed by his pale thin lips.

"Is something wrong?"

"Your teeth. I wasn't ready for them. They aren't like the others'...."

"I am not like the others, nor is Eldritch. We are a separate race entirely. And yes, he does have wings."

Poe nodded and poured boiling water into the mugs. "You take sugar and milk?"

"Alright."

He added milk and sugar to both coffees and carried the mugs over, handing one to Nivek. The cup looked more like a shot glass in Nivek's huge, clawed hands.

"So what are you then?"

"I used to be an angel."

Poe's eyebrows went up as he settled into an old overstuffed armchair. He could still feel the bass through the floor from his club downstairs despite the thousands of dollars-worth of soundproofing he'd had installed to prevent noise leakage. But now he had something else to think about.

"An angel?"

Nivek nodded and sipped at his coffee, grimacing slightly at the bitter sweetness of the liquid. "Before the battle."

"I see."

"It was nothing personal."

Poe stared at the fallen angel for a moment. If he looked close enough, he could still see some of the beauty left over from angelic features. The pale white skin stretched tightly over chiseled features accentuated the silver eyes with their black lashes and somewhat thick eyebrows while the wide, thin lips held a slight upward curve to them. All in all, Nivek had a fiercely friendly face, Poe supposed.

"So... now you're a demon?"

"Somewhat. In order to be called to physical servitude my master had to supply me with a physical body. I am part human." Nivek paused, staring into his coffee, "I cannot say I've enjoyed the experience. Humanity is, as your species says, a 'pain in the ass.'"

Poe burst out laughing, causing Nivek to smile in confusion. "Have I said something amusing?"

Poe nodded at the demon, continuing to laugh. "I didn't expect you to know words like that—or phrases. I guess I'd hoped Hell hadn't been corrupted by American metaphors."

Nivek smiled. "Americans are a majority there, but I think you have the wrong idea of Hell."

Poe's eyebrows went up again. "Do tell."

"It is not a place of punishment as humans believe. It is a place of conscience above all else. In Hell one has a very long time to contemplate one's actions and either accept and repent, or... well... sometimes we never learn our lessons, do we?"

Poe nodded, becoming grave as he set his coffee on an endtable. "Tell me something, Nivek."

"What would you like to know?"

'Why did you side with the... well, with

Lucifer? You seem like a nice guy and all. So why fight God?"

Nivek smiled sadly as he set his barely-touched coffee on the table. His silver eyes stared far away, as if through time. "Humans are not the only creatures that can succumb to temptation and seduction. Angels can be just as impulsive."

"I see."

Nivek shrugged and got to his feet. "No one is perfect. I thank you for your time and for the... coffee. It has been a pleasure."

"But now to business?" Poe offered and the demon nodded.

They walked back down to the dancefloor and Nivek motioned to a cage with a thin brunette.

"She will be suitable. How much would you like for her?"

"I'll give her to you for a thousand tonight. That good?"

"Very. Thank you." Nivek handed him the

money and Poe looked to Carlos. His partner stared at him and then at Nivek, frowning slightly.

"Excuse me a moment, Nivek. I need to talk to Carlos."

"Be careful," the demon warned, "your lover is extremely jealous at the moment."

"Jealous?"

"He believes that you and I have engaged in sexual acts while absent from the main floor."

Poe smiled and shook his head. "That's ridiculous! He knows I'd never do that! I love him... I'll be right back."

He pushed his way through the crowd, making his way up to where the Phreak glared down.

"Hey, what's wrong?"

Carlos crossed his arms and his frown deepened. "Where the hell'd you go?"

"Just up for coffee."

"Bullshit. You were gone way too long for

just coffee."

"Carlos, you know I'd never do that... hey, I love *you*, remember?"

"He ain't bad looking, either. Hell, I'd do him."

"Carlos! Jesus, what's gotten into you? Huh? Hey, come here, please." He tried to take Carlos into his arms, tried to kiss him, but he pulled away. "Dammit, he's just a CLIENT! He's friends with that other guy that comes here, you know, the one with the wings?"

Carlos turned to him finally and Poe inwardly sighed with relief. He didn't want to lose his best friend, partner, and lover all in the same night because he'd invited a demon up for coffee. He smiled at Carlos and took him into his arms.

"I love you, Carl. I do. And I don't ever want to lose you, OK?"

"I guess so. But you never took a client upstairs before."

Poe hugged Carlos tighter. "I just had a weird feeling that he needed to talk to someone. And I was right. Did you know he's a demon? I think him and his buddy with the wings live in that old haunted church. Those two are our best customers and I wouldn't want to lose them, either."

"Alright, I'm sorry."

Carlos pulled back and lowered the brunette to the dancefloor. He had tears in his eyes. "Guess I got carried away."

Poe grabbed him and kissed him, then smoothed his hair as he held him. "Shh. I'm sorry I upset you. I didn't mean to. You can come meet him if it'll make you feel better."

Carlos nodded against his shoulder and wiped at his eyes while Poe held back his own tears. He hated it when Carlos cried. It made him want to crawl under a rock and die. It also made him jealous of his lover's ability to express his emotions freely. He looked across the dancefloor and motioned for Nivek to come up.

The demon was in front of them almost instantly, brunette in hand. "She should last slightly longer than the others," Nivek told them quietly. "She somewhat resembles his wife."

Poe nodded understanding, then made introductions, "Nivek, this is Carlos. Carlos, Nivek."

Phreak stared at Nivek sullenly for a moment, then looked to Poe, who nodded. Reluctantly he shook hands.

"I thank you for the coffee and the girl, Mr. Ellison," Nivek said, then to Carlos, "I am sorry you were upset. Perhaps next time we will all have coffee together?"

Carlos visibly relaxed and managed a sincere smile at the demon. "Yes. I'd like that very much."

Nivek made a short bow to the two men and carried the woman away neatly tucked under his trenchcoat. Poe turned to Carlos and smiled. "See? Just coffee."

Carlos smiled and nodded, then briefly

checked his watch. "Almost time to close up."

Poe checked his own watch and his eyebrows shot up. "Almost five! Jesus. They're here late tonight."

Carlos nodded as he began to slowly bring up the lights. Most of their "merchandise" was sold except for a tall, muscular blond man. He had been the hardest to acquire. He'd come to the Hanging Cages looking for a job as a bouncer. Carlos had somehow managed to get him into one of the cages and he was up there now, still clothed, not blindfolded, gagged, or tied. It would be one huge fuck-up if he got loose. Lucky for them the guy was terrified of heights, not to mention he'd be seriously hurt if he tried to jump the fifty feet to the floor.

As the club emptied and the first rays of sunrise began to penetrate the cracks in the boarded-up windows the man in the cage began to yell.

"Hey! Let me down! You hear me, faggot? Let me down! I don't want the job, OK? Are you listening to me? I swear, when I get down, I'm going to beat the shit out of both your queer asses!"

Poe walked to the middle of the floor and smiled up at his prisoner. Then, in a high-pitched falsetto with an exaggerated lisp he called back to Carlos, "Oooh! Look at him! …He's ssooo dreamy. Can I have him for Chrissmass?" He clapped his hands and fanned himself, grinning over at his lover.

"You Goddamfaggotqueerass!!! Let me out of here and we'll see who's laughing," the blond man panted, his knuckles white as he gripped the bars and his face pale with homophobic fury.

"Shut up, asshole, or I'll tear you open and leave your insides spread out as an appetizer for our clients."

Blondie finally took the hint and cringed in the corner of the cage. Poe shook his head in disgust as he took Carlos by the hand. He'd feel much better when they finally sold the asshole.

"We should really tie him up."

Carlos nodded.

"We'll wait until he falls asleep, maybe even drug him, then we'll get him ready for sale."

Again Carlos nodded and Poe turned to him. "What's wrong, Carl?"

"I don't like what he said."

"Neither do I. That's why I want him sold. To someone mean."

"What about Nivek?"

Poe grinned and took Carlos in his arms. "You're a genius, as always."

They waited for Blondie to fall asleep, then carefully lowered the cage. The large man stirred slightly and Poe placed a cloth soaked in chloroform over the man's mouth.

"Easy there, Brighteyes," Poe grinned and Carlos handed him duct tape, scissors, and two pairs of handcuffs.

They fastened the two pairs of shackles already in the cage to the man's wrists and ankles, then put an extra set of cuffs on each wrist. Poe placed a strip of duct tape over the man's mouth and they were set. Now for the undressing.

Carlos handed him the scissors and Poe cut down the sleeves of the man's dress shirt. He was probably an office-worker by the look of him; hair neatly cropped in a high and tight police-style cut and face at one point clean-shaven. Poe cut away the shirt and sneered. The guy was buff, but he had breasts. Carlos giggled and held out the man's driver's license.

"Rob? Jesus, what a damned name. Where's Barbie, Ken?"

Carlos pulled off their prisoner's shoes and socks while Poe unfastened the belt and cut away the pants. Both men burst out laughing.

"No underwear," Carlos laughed, "and even less of a dick."

Poe shook his head. "Steroids... Jesus, what an idiot."

Carlos suppressed his laughter for a moment

to add, "And the chicks probably look at him and think he's all that 'til they get him in bed."

Poe snorted. "Assuming there's no lights on and he can actually get them into bed without them laughing. I've heard of shortcomings, but this is ridiculous."

They laughed at the joke and then Poe took the duct tape from Carlos. "Time for Sleeping Booby to wake up. Has it been enough time?"

Carlos shrugged. "You know, time flies," he said with a smile.

Poe smiled and ran strips of duct tape over Rob's chest. The hair was just long enough for their next action to be potentially excruciating. They stepped back, admiring the sight of future agony for a moment, then Carlos grabbed the tape.

"What are you doing?" Poe laughed.

"Watch." Carlos stuck a strip over the man's pubic hair, pressing it firmly into place, then put another strip over the scrotum. Poe bent over laughing and Carlos shrugged. "Now he has a reason to hate us… or at least he *will* have a reason."

They sat and stared at their prisoner for a few agonizing minutes before Poe finally got up. "Hell, this'll take forever. Fuck it." He gripped a corner of one of the strips of tape on the man's chest and pulled. Rob woke up. Screaming.

"Don't ever insult us again," Poe whispered savagely as he grabbed the second strip and pulled.

Rob howled behind his duct tape gag and Poe smiled. "And you haven't even been introduced to my partner here," he said through clenched teeth, "After he's through with you you'll know why we call him The Phreak." Then, turning to Carlos, "He's all yours."

Carlos reached out to the remaining strips of duct tape across the man's genitals, and with the psychotic grin of a pure sadist, he pulled.

Later, after Rob had stopped screaming, they decided to pay a call on Nivek and try to sell their unwilling guest. Poe stared out of the window thoughtfully.

"So how do you know where Nivek lives?" Carlos asked from behind him.

Poe shrugged. "I don't. Not really. But I have this feeling that he's in the old abandoned church not far from here."

Carlos nodded, considering the idea. "You may be right. I think I saw someone looking out the window of the tower on the place. Big guy, creepy as hell. Could've been Nivek."

Poe turned to him, a small smile curling his lips. "Let's go drop by for coffee."

The two men stood outside of the old cathedral, holding each other's hand tightly in mute fear. It wasn't yet sunset and the sky was overcast as the autumn wind blew the dead limbs of summer beyond the rusted gates. Carlos was the first to break the silence.

"I don't like it, man. Gives me the fucking willies, like this old haunted factory in Jersey City near where I grew up. Kids'd dare each other to go in and some never came out, y'know?"

Poe nodded as he contemplated the looming structure before them. Carlos was right, this place *was* creepy. Reluctantly they moved past the statues of gargoyles and reached the door.

Carlos let out a small whistle and Poe stared at the carvings on the door in amazement. They looked like ancient writings.

"What the hell does it say?"

Poe shrugged numbly. "Damned if I know."

The streetlamps began to buzz with light as the last rays of sunset spread over New York City's sky like a slow fire. Both men jumped at the sound of movement behind them.

"Good evening, gentlemen. Can we help you with anything?"

Poe and Carlos both turned to find Eldritch along with about half a dozen other gargoyles staring at them with golden, glowing eyes.

"Yeah... we're here to see Nivek," Poe finally managed to get out after the initial shock of seeing Eldritch without his disguise. Not only did he have wings, but he had fangs and claws, too.

"Follow me." The gargoyle pushed past them and into the darkness inside the cathedral. They found Nivek carrying the body of the brunette from the night before out of the tower room. He didn't seem surprised to see them.

"Greetings once more. I regret that I was wrong about this poor girl lasting longer than the others... at least she has not been mutilated."

They stared collectively at the brunette, her pretty features smooth and peaceful in death. Nivek shrugged in disappointment and glanced to Eldritch.

"These are our new friends, Eldritch. Meet Mr. Ellison and Mr. Mendoza. Gentlemen, this is Eldritch."

They briefly shook hands after Nivek had set the brunette's body down in a corner, taking care to cover the corpse with a sheet. He and Eldritch stared at the closed door. The sound of heavy, impatient footsteps could be heard coming from the other side of the wood.

"Is that your master?" Poe asked and Nivek raised a quick finger to his lips, nodding.

"Yes," Eldritch whispered, "That is Nemesis."

"Nemesis?" Poe and Carlos exclaimed simultaneously. "Jesus H., Nivek! You didn't tell me that that was who your master was!" Poe stammered.

"Would you not have helped me, then?"

"Nivek…. God. Nemesis is the man to fear! They'd have killed him if they could have found him. Chrissakes, he started the fucking Immortal War!"

Nivek nodded gravely as he led them back down the corridor, away from the door. "Allow me to show you the only reason that Eldritch and I have stayed on here."

They stopped outside a set of ornately carved

double doors and Nivek and Eldritch hung their heads almost out of habit before Nivek pushed the doors open. "Guilt and love are powerful forces, gentlemen," the demon told them quietly.

"Especially when they are both contained in one act," the gargoyle added as they entered the bedchamber of the mistress of the house.

"Oh my God… she's beautiful," Carlos breathed.

"She's… dead."

The demon and gargoyle nodded miserably.

"But she will only be dead for a short time," Nivek said hopefully.

"Unfortunately, *he*," Eldritch motioned toward the direction of the tower, "will also be free when she is."

As if on cue Nemesis began to throw things and yell for release. Nivek ran a hand across his tired eyes.

"Nemesis is not easily taken care of. He

must be the one to wake up Lamia, or she will remember nothing of us, or of what she is."

"Or even *who* she is," Eldritch finished. Poe would have almost smiled at the way the demon and gargoyle hit the conversation back and forth like a verbal tennis match, but this game had no winners.

Nivek moved to the side of the bed where Lamia lay, dressed (or shrouded?) in white from head to toe. She would have made a beautiful picture, the way her long, glossy black hair curled over the pillows, accentuating her pale, almost alabaster skin. Her eyes would have been gorgeous when open. Poe envied her long, lush black lashes and her small, pink, almost doll-like mouth. Even in death she seemed to be smiling. A living picture of a dead Mona Lisa.

The picture had its flaws, of course. Like the bloody stake protruding from where her heart would have been. Poe closed his eyes and shook his head sadly.

"What a waste."

Nivek looked at him for a second then nodded agreement. They stared in silence at Lamia for a moment longer and then Nivek ushered them from the room, gently closing the door behind them. When he looked at them again, his eyes seemed to glow in the darkness.

"I do not expect that you both have come to speak of the dead with Eldritch and me. Would you like to discuss your proposition over some coffee?"

Poe smiled and followed the demon and gargoyle to the huge expanse of a kitchen. Poe and Carlos took a seat while Nivek put some water on to boil and Eldritch got the cups.

"Well?" Nivek asked, turning to lean his upper thigh on the top of the counter.

"We got this guy," Poe started.

"And we want to get his ass gone," Carlos finished. A look of deep-seated rage burned in his usually gentle brown eyes and he smacked his long golden fingers on the tabletop. "And we want it done slow and painful."

"Can you help us?"

Nivek glanced to Eldritch and the two started to smile. The demon turned back to face them, his smile wider than before. "It is a man?"

They nodded.

"You wish him a painful death?"

Again they nodded.

"Bring him to us."

"Well, see, that's the whole problem. The guy's huge. Are you sure Nemesis can handle someone like that?"

Nivek smiled and motioned for them to follow him, the coffee forgotten. He led them back up to the tower, closer to the noises that emanated from behind the door. He and Eldritch stood on either side of the door, tensed and ready, then Nivek opened the door.

"Holy shit," Carlos whispered, "he's even bigger in real life."

Nemesis turned at the sound, couch poised

over his head and ready for flight. A look of crazed curiosity filled his emerald green gaze and a small bemused smile twitched at the corners of his wide harsh mouth. He dropped the couch and his smile widened.

"Well, Nivek, this is new meat. Afraid the women weren't enough for me?"

Nemesis grinned and walked toward them with slow panther-strides. His long black hair moved like spider legs around his hollowly handsome face and his mouth twisted into a harsh smile.

"They are not for you, Nemesis," Nivek said flatly. "These two gentlemen are your providers. You should thank them for your survival."

Nemesis arched an eyebrow and his smile grew. "Oh, forgive me, boys."

"You're the one who started the war," Poe stated and Nemesis nodded proudly.

He stood in the doorway now, just within arm's reach of the small group gathered in the hallway outside. He stood well over six feet tall,

Poe guessed, maybe even seven feet. He was dressed completely in black, and his features were sharply chiseled and angular. And he watched them like a predator.

"So…," Nemesis grinned and crossed his arms over his wide chest. "Why would two evolved monkeys want to help me?"

"We didn't know it was for you," Poe said flatly. He didn't like Nemesis when he'd seen him in the news broadcasts at the beginning of the Immortal War, and he didn't like him now that he was talking to him. Not at all.

"I see." The smile seemed to falter on Nemesis's lips. "And now that you know you refuse to help?"

"No. We'll help, but not for you."

The smile was gone now, and Nemesis's eyes glittered coldly as they stared at Poe. "I believe it's time for dinner, Nivek. Where is the virgin sacrifice for tonight, hmm?"

Nivek turned to Poe and Carlos. "I think we can solve your problem, gentlemen, and maybe feed ours for at least one more night." The demon sighed heavily and glared over his shoulder at Nemesis. "I wish it were so easy to rid ourselves of our torment."

"I heard that, Nivek."

"I am pleased that you did, Nemesis. It has been over ten years since your foolishness. Ten years of killing innocents." Nivek turned to face his master and growled, "And I am weary of cleaning up your messes."

"Bring me better women and you won't have to keep cleaning them up." Nemesis laughed. "They just don't breed them like they used to."

"Let's go, Nivek," Poe said flatly. "I need you to remind me again of why I should help him."

Nemesis pressed as close to the door as he dared and the wood frame sent off sparks of electricity at his nearness. The smile covering his face was less than friendly.

"I'll remind you," Nemesis growled, his green eyes boring into Poe before coming to rest on Carlos, "You're helping me because when I get out of here I might let you live, or at least make your death quick and painless."

Poe grabbed Carlos's hand and pulled him away from Nemesis's psychotic stare. "Come on. We're getting out of here."

Nivek ushered them through the corridors while Eldritch closed the door to Nemesis's screamed obscenities and insults.

Carlos cast a fearful glance backward and said, "He was hot, but damn, what a psycho."

Poe nodded gravely, able to appreciate his lover's taste in men. Nemesis looked like a black-clad god, but he was completely dangerous. He looked into Carlos's frightened eyes and tried to summon a smile.

"You don't think he was serious, do you?" Carlos asked after a pause. They followed Nivek to the doors of the master bedroom.

Poe looked at his lover and his brow furrowed in confusion. "How do you mean?"

"You don't think he could really get out of there, do you?"

The thought hadn't even crossed Poe's mind, but now he felt a lump of numb fear filling his stomach. He opened his mouth and no words came out.

Instead, Nivek answered for him, "Nemesis will never escape as long as Eldritch and I stay on as his caretakers. Many have already tried to free him, but we quickly dispensed with them."

"You mean you killed the people who tried to free Nemesis? Does he know?"

Nivek smirked at Poe and opened the doors to the Mistress's chamber. "No. And he never will. Lamia is safer this way. At least the current situation keeps her out of harm's way."

Carlos stared at Lamia's peacefully impaled form and ran a slender golden hand over his hair. His jaw muscles worked beneath the skin and he looked to Nivek. "You said Lamia. Is that her name?"

The demon nodded as Eldritch joined them.

"I've heard of her… she was pretty popular in the music world a long time ago and then she disappeared for a while and came back. When she disappeared again everyone assumed she was taking a break from the war scene, but she stayed gone for so long they figured she was killed. *Is* she dead?"

Nivek cast an uneasy glance to Eldritch and shrugged. "We are not certain. All we know is that she will be resurrected when the stake is removed."

Carlos nodded and touched Lamia's cheek gently, but Poe was unsatisfied with the answer.

"So she wakes up when the stake's removed? Why not pull it out then?"

Carlos quickly pulled his hand away as if he had been burned, exclaiming, "Jesus! She's cold as ice!"

"If we were to pull out the stake ourselves,

then Lamia would not remember who or what she is. Nemesis must pull it out in order to restore her to her true self."

Poe looked at Lamia's sleeping form, following the gentle lines of her face and neck to the slopes of her breasts. There the continuity was disrupted by the jagged stake and patches of long-dried blood spotting the immaculate white of her dress.

"But isn't she in pain?" he asked distantly. He looked to Nivek for an answer and the demon and gargoyle both dropped their eyes.

"We are unsure of that as well."

Two nights passed before they saw Nivek and Eldritch again. They both rushed into the pulsing beat of the club and up to the soundbooth where Poe and Carlos stood. They had been unable to move their large guest safely to his final resting place due to increased police activity in the area, and business had suffered considerably.

"We need your help," Nivek panted, gripping the edge of the soundbooth for support.

"What's up?" Poe asked uneasily. He didn't like seeing supernatural beings upset, especially when these two happened to be the ones keeping the destroyer of humanity locked away in his prison.

"Lamia is awake."

Poe's eyes widened. Apparently their little discussion had hit home somewhere. "What? But how? I thought—."

Nivek held up a hand. "We never said it could not be accomplished. We were merely unsure of the complete results. She could be awakened by another, and has been." With that the demon glared over at Eldritch with accusing eyes and the gargoyle shifted guiltily. "She has no memory of what she is."

"Does that mean Nemesis is free, too?" Carlos asked fearfully.

Eldritch quickly shook his head. "No. He remains imprisoned."

"Presently we need blood for Lamia so that she may heal. We have brought containers to hold it, but we must leave the corpse here in order to insure Lamia's peace of mind. Can you help us?"

Poe nodded and Carlos worked the controls to lower the cage with Rob in it to the floor. As if sensing the charge in the air, the crowd moved silently out of the way so they could gain easier access to their prisoner. The dancefloor was quiet except for the man in the cage. He was weak from starvation, but he still managed to put up one hell of a fight when he saw what waited for him.

The four of them dragged him kicking and screaming to a back alley where they quickly slashed his throat and drained his blood into several winebottles. When the bottles had been filled, they dragged him back inside, weak, but still alive.

Carlos climbed into the soundbooth and turned on the mic while Poe set up an antique table in the center of the dancefloor. Nivek and Eldritch dropped the limp body on the table and Poe ripped away the duct tape covering Rob's eyes and mouth as Carlos's deep, slightly accented voice boomed over the PA.

"Hey all, you'll notice we got a freebie on the floor there. Help yourselves and accept it as a token of our appreciation for your continued patronage. And take your time and enjoy him, we won't mind."

Poe smirked down at their weakened victim, but Rob's pale eyes didn't show any signs of dread at the Phreak's open invitation to live dinner, so Poe broke open some smelling salts and held them under Rob's broken nose.

"Fuck!" he bellowed as full awareness settled into his gaze.

He sat up and stared around him blearily as the crowd closed in like sharks on blood.

Poe held up his hands and said to the mob, "I want it slow and painful for this asshole, you got it?

I want his death to make my stomach turn. Go ahead."

With that he moved out of the way and the throng fell on the large man with howls of ecstasy and hunger. Poe nodded farewell to Nivek and Eldritch and turned to join Carlos in the soundbooth. From there he and Carlos watched the carnage below and held hands. Rob was torn to shreds, the crowd drinking what remaining blood was left, fangs glistening red in the limelight.

"What say we retire, Carl? Move somewhere far away."

"Why?"

"I just have a feeling that something bad's going to happen."

"You mean Nemesis."

Poe nodded. "He'll get out. There was a loophole with Lamia, why not with Nemesis, too? And when he escapes, he's going to kill us. So let's get out of here before that happens. We've got enough to retire on and live huge if we wanted to.

I'm getting tired of the business. And we took care of our buddy Rob. You in?"

Carlos nodded. "Yeah, I think you're right. We've been lucky this whole time anyway. Only a matter of time before the pigs catch on...."

They stared down at the murder beneath them, watching as a blood-smeared hand reached desperately out of the pile of writhing bodies.

"Think he suffered?" Carlos asked in a distant voice.

His eyes shone with bloodlust and vengeance. A small smile danced at the corners of his mouth.

"Still is," Poe grinned.

OF POISONS AND CURES

by

Suzi M.

Drip.

drip.

Drip.

drip.

Crimson splashing the immaculate white tiles, pooling around the paling outstretched fingertips.

Drip.

drip.

Drip.

drip.

The bath water cold now. Cold as the bather, lips blue and fallen slightly open, blue eyes glazing at the faucet. Drip drip. Drip drip.

The eyes blinked and fingers twitched as breathing grew more and more shallow, as shallow as the cold pink-red water in the bathtub. Shallow as the blood pool on the floor. White tiles graying, growing fainter, less defined as they shattered out of focus. Dry tongue struggled over dry lips, the faint and labored breathing echoing off the bathroom walls to the Drip-drip backbeat.

A tentative knock at the door.

Drip drip.

"Are you almost done? I have to use the bathroom."

Dead eyes rolled upwards and closed. The faint breathing exhaled and ended.

Drip drip.

"Hey, come on. I *know* you're in there."

A nervous pause and another, somewhat louder knock.

Drip drip. Drop. Razor blade falling from dead fingers into the crimson puddle, bouncing onto the red-soaked bathmat. The knocking on the door became louder, more insistent and almost panicked.

"Andrew? Andy, are you OK in there?"

The man stood over him and shook his head in regret. "I'm disappointed in you, Andrew." He shrugged and smirked. "I had some hope for you. And she really *did* love you."

"Sweetie? Honey, please open the door…. You're scaring me now."

He could see, the glazed film covering his eyes was starting to clear again.

"You have a choice," the man told him, pale red lips drawing back from strange teeth. Andrew decided he could definitely do without this guy and his weird silver eyes.

"What choice do I have at this point? I thought I made my last one a little while ago.... Didn't I?

The man seemed to laugh at him silently before replying, "No. I am in a generous mood today. I will give you the choice of life or death."

Andrew stared down at his body, framed in blood and pale as it shriveled in the water. He heard the faraway sound of a key in the lock and then his mother practically fell into the bathroom. A shaking hand flew to her mouth, which was pulled back into a silent scream of horror. Sudden remorse filled him and he looked down. He missed his body already.

"Well?"

He glanced up at the man in sudden understanding. "I thought Death was supposed to be some bright light or a skeleton in a cloak with a big sickle or something."

Now the man openly laughed at him while below them Andrew's mother screamed finally began to scream, so very far away. "I oblige those who are dying on occasion. Or if it is not truly their time. And it is called a *scythe*, not 'a big sickle'," the Angel of Death chuckled, resting thin elbows on black slacks as he sat on thin air. Death in a white dress shirt and black slacks with silver eyes; it was too much for Andrew to even begin to fathom. He had his own demise to consider now, after all.

"You know, now that I've actually thought it over...," Andrew paused, staring at the man's—at *Death*'s—paper-white features contrasted by neatly cropped raven-black hair. Before he had died it had seemed like such a logical choice, and he had acted on it. Now he wasn't sure at all. A name came into his head and he spoke it aloud, "Azrael?"

"Yes." The silver eyes stared into his while Andrew took a moment to process this new information. Death had a name, and it was the name of a cartoon villain's cat. Dear God, this was getting stranger by the minute. Andrew would have laughed, but somehow it didn't seem appropriate with his mother crying below them, holding his dead (or dying?) body in her arms and the Angel of Death staring at him.

"What will happen to me if I go back?"

Azrael shrugged, his angelic mouth curling into a twisted smile. "That is all up to you. Make your decision before those you love make one for you."

Andrew ran a hand through his longish blond hair and sighed.

"Well?" asked the Angel of Death.

"I never figured you for an advocate of free will. I thought it was all planned out for us or something." He looked at Death and the angel shrugged, starting to look impatient. "It's going to be the same when I go back. They don't understand me—"

"I am not here to act as your mental and emotional advisor," Azrael told him impatiently, "I am beginning to regret my generosity."

Andrew frowned and fidgeted nervously. "Well… then I choose to live."

"So be it," Azrael said and walked away.

He woke in the hospital, surrounded by more white, his wrists stitched and bandaged, and restrained at his sides, an IV connected to a drip bag. Andrew blinked up at the concerned faces surrounding him and offered a dizzy smile. They all let their breath out collectively, as if they had been waiting for the moment he opened his eyes.

"Andy?" his ex-girlfriend's brown eyes stared into his helplessly. Guiltily.

"We were so *worried*," his mother's tired voice told him from the other side of the bed, "They say you were dead for a little bit…." Her voice died in a series of choked sobs. She looked so much older than she had the last time he had seen her. Her hair seemed to have more gray in it, and the fine lines that had been forming around her eyes had deepened to the permanent lines of a worried parent.

Andrew felt his own choked sobs rising in the back of his throat. Mainly for his mother. He didn't give a damn about his ex. Not anymore. His mother raised swollen red eyes to meet his and tried to smile trough her tears.

"I'll go get the doctor," she whispered as she gave a gentle squeeze to his hand, then covered her face and rushed from the room. He could hear her choked sobs in the hallway and he stared after her until a touch to his hand made him turn. His ex-girlfriend smiled miserably at him.

"Hi, Andy."

"Hi."

"I—I came as soon as I heard about it... you know," she motioned to his wrists and dropped her eyes quickly. "Oh, Andy, I'm so sorry...."

"For what?" Only anger and annoyance were evident in his voice. He felt an inward satisfaction at the guilt and surprise he saw in her eyes. He had never spoken to her in the way he was now. Once he had loved her, *worshipped* her. The way her hair would catch the morning sun, turning it to spun gold brought tears to his eyes. And the day he had walked in on her and his best friend... *that* had brought tears to his eyes as well.

"I never thought you would do anything like this," she gently held his bandaged wrist as is he were unaware of what he had done to himself and he shook her off as much as the restraints would allow. He almost laughed at her, but the joke wasn't that funny anymore.

"You think I did this because of *you*? I wouldn't waste my life on something so trashy." He felt only a sadist's enjoyment when her eyes filled with tears. "Get out, Toni. I think you've done enough to both of us."

"Andy—"

"Out. Now. I'm not going to even bother giving you forgiveness for what you've done, since you never even had the decency to treat me like a human while we were together. You and Eric can rot in hell for all I care, and I hope you do."

"You don't mean that—"

"Oh, yes I do. And I'll tell you what else. You're a whore. You think with your twat and not your heart or head. So much for promises made in the dark, right, bitch?"

"Fuck you," she spat as Andrew's ex-best friend walked in. Toni looked to Eric briefly, then back to Andrew. "Do us all a favor and stay dead next time."

"Do Eric a favor and get tested."

She stared at him as if she were going to slap him if not punch him, and Eric's jaw dropped.

Andrew sneered. "Go ahead, show Eric what you're really like and hit a half-dead man who's chained to the bed. That's so classic you." He turned to look at Eric and his smile melted to something far uglier. "And what about you, buddy? You want to get a shot in, too? Or would my back be more your style?"

"Hey now—"

"Shut up. I have nothing more to say to either one of you. Hope you enjoy her. The best things in life really are cheap, right?" Andrew's smile was a deranged frown now, and he went on, "Now both of you get out of my second chance at life."

His mother came in with the doctor at the moment Toni and Eric were leaving. Perfect timing, thought Andrew. She walks in on the end of my life, and now she walks in on the ending of my friendships with the two people who meant the most to me at one time. That was before I died.

"How are you feeling, Andy?" the doctor asked him.

Andrew, he thought angrily, my name is *Andrew* not Andy, damn it. "I'm OK, I guess," he said out loud. The doctor looked over Andrew's chart and frowned slightly while Andrew's mother nervously looked on.

"Little run-in with a razor… you're lucky to be alive."

"I made my decision."

"You almost didn't have that choice," the doctor said, staring at him gravely from over the clipboard. "You will have to be spending some time in the mental ward, you understand. Until we can verify that you won't be trying any of this," he motioned to Andrew's wrists, "again." The gray eyes stared holes into Andrew's soul from under thick black eyebrows.

"I kind of figured," Andrew told him, meeting his gaze levelly, deciding to keep his mouth shut about the tunnel of light, and of course about Azrael.

"Good. Get used to people watching over you shoulder for a long time, Andy."

Andrew fought the urge to stick his tongue out at the doctor's back as he left the room, leaving Andrew's mother behind to flounder through conversation attempts.

"Doctor Vitalis says you were…," her voice trailed off as her eyes filled with tears again and she couldn't finish the sentence—the *word*.

"Dead?" Andrew tried helpfully. This only made her cry harder and he felt bad. And angry. All the times he had tried to tell her what was wrong and she had brushed him off for lawn parties and tea with The Girls. He hated to admit it, but his mother, with her graying head of red-blonde hair and neurotic ways, was as shallow as the average bathtub. She and all of her friends could have stuffed a mattress with all of the fluff they housed in their No Diving heads. She wiped at her aging tired eyes and blinked at him.

"It was my fault, wasn't it?" she asked him wretchedly. She twisted her handkerchief in her veined hands while he stared at her in surprise.

"No, Mom. It wasn't your fault," he shrugged and tried to think of the right words. Ironic, he should be the one getting comforted and here he was comforting her.

"There was just so much sh—" he censored himself when his mother looked at him in surprise— "just so many bad things going on, you know?" The Would-Be Dead comforting the Almost Living.

"Was it really that bad?"

"Yes."

"Oh," she dropped her swollen eyes. "Well… why don't I go get something for us to eat, and you can get some rest." She tried to smile and ended up breaking into tears. Andrew felt his heart pull at the sight of her.

"Go get some rest, Mom," he told her gently, wishing he wasn't restrained so he could comfort her. Almost as an afterthought he added quietly, "I love you."

"I love you, too," she whispered. She seemed to be surprised by his words, and he guessed she should be. Neither one of them had told the other that they loved them since he was a kid and still needed a nightlight.

When she turned to leave she nearly walked over the doctor… what was his name? Vital-something… Vitalis. Andrew hadn't even noticed the guy come into the room.

"Hello, Mrs. Desmond."

"Oh! Dr. Vitalis… oh my. I didn't even hear you come in," his mother's hand fluttered to rest over her heart and she fanned herself nervously.

"Please, call me David," he told her and Andrew blinked in astonishment. If he didn't know better he'd swear this guy was hitting on his *mother*, who could easily have been "David's" mother, too from the looks of it. And his mother seemed to be eating it up.

"And you may call me Beverly, … David. What is that name's origin? I don't think I've ever heard it before…. It's lovely."

"It's Greek as far as I know. It means 'immortal'." Dr. David Vitalis? Andrew rolled his eyes and cleared his throat noisily. His mother blinked, reluctantly pulling her gaze from please-call-me-David's eyes. She glanced around, searching and confused, almost disoriented. "Well, I seem to have forgotten what it was I was on my way to do…." She laughed, embarrassment evident on her face.

"You were going to get some food, and then going to get some rest," Andrew reminded her. Both his mother and the doctor glanced at him in a way that gave him the distinct impression that they wished he weren't there to interrupt the conversation. Andrew didn't care. This David the immortal guy wasn't getting paid vast amounts of money to hit on his mom, he was getting paid to take care of the sick, injured, and dying—not necessarily in that order. His mother—oh, sorry, she was now Beverly, not *Mom*, hi, I-could-be-yours, too, David, whoever she was attempting to be at the moment—she wasn't helping the situation. She seemed to be searching for a reason to stay in the room now, where only minutes ago she had wanted out.

"Doc—I mean, David," she giggled like a

middle-aged schoolgirl when Doctor Love raised a halting eyebrow, "What brought you back here again so soon? Don't you have other rounds to make? … Medicine to give…?"

"Indeed I do, Beverly. But I don't actually administer the meds—medications most of the time. I prescribe a drug and the nurses take it from there. I came here because I feel your boy is well enough to take a little ride to Fourth—the mental ward." He quickly added when 'Beverly' started to tear up again, "He'll be out and about soon enough. I assure you." The doctor d'amour never took his gray eyes from momma lovemuffin during his entire speech. Andrew felt himself becoming ill at the thought of his mother as the object of a young man's lust. His mother wasn't really all that old, probably the same age as the doctor, but the point was that she was his *mother*. Had Andrew really stopped to consider it, he would have realized that what he was experiencing was jealousy, but for now he was just being a good, protective son who felt that after a suicide attempt— almost successful, he might add—he wasn't asking too much when all he wanted was their undivided attention.

They continued to stare at one another and Andrew said, "Should I leave the room so you two can be alone?" A bit loud, a bit obnoxious, a bit accusatory, a lot successful. The two adults jumped like a couple of teenagers caught necking in the school parking lot on prom night. Doctor Immortal Love-Stud smiled at him, but the stormy gray eyes held another, more menacing emotion in their clouded depths and Andrew began to feel uneasy. Like maybe he should have never fucked with this guy.

"Your boy has a great sense of humor," the doctor chuckled, but Andrew could hear the anger under the laughter. "He's going to need it on the Fourth Floor."

Now Andrew's mother was laughing delightedly as if the man had just made some wonderful joke instead of a thinly veiled threat. She never took her wide eyes from the doctor, never once looked at her son during the journey to the mental ward. It was almost like she'd been drugged or hypnotized, but would it have been possible to do that without Andrew noticing?

"Well, here you are, Andy. Your new home away from home."

Andrew looked to his doctor's gloating stare and then to the fourth floor mental ward. It *looked* like a mental ward. And for the criminally insane it seemed. Bars were everywhere, and Andrew wondered if their function was to hold the patients in, or keep the rest of the world out.

Everything was plaster-white, including the bars. Even the daylight coming through the barred and metal-reinforced glass windows seemed to lack the yellow glowing warmth of sunlight. The place was cold and completely unfriendly as they approached the barred door of the entrance.

"We have to keep our security way up," Dr. David told them casually, "especially with the customer we've recently acquired. Paranoid schizophrenic, homicidal psychopath. Already killed a few guards trying to get out of here. Don't blame him, really. This place can get crazy sometimes."

Andrew's mother went into nearly hysterical laughter and it took good ole David a moment to realize he'd made a funny. And not a very good one. It was short-lived humor, shattered by the sounds of a struggle and then howls of rage that didn't sound anywhere near to human. A chill gripped Andrew's heart and refused to let go as Doctor Call-Me-David Vitalis walked up to the barred door to announce Andrew Desmond's arrival. He was still pissed to notice his mother's gaze following the doctor's every move like a lovesick schoolgirl.

"Nice place here, isn't it, Mom?"

"Yes, it is," she answered distantly. At that point Andrew figured she'd have agreed to just about anything, even the existence of "real" vampires and their cause that they currently fought for in the larger cities of the world.

The shouts were getting closer. Andrew

blinked as he came out of his wanderings and noticed the huge white-clad form rushing toward the bars of the door. At first the guy looked like he should have been one of the guards; he was enormous, pushing seven feet tall easily and carrying the muscle to back it up. He shoved through the growing crowd of hospital staff as they tried to block his escape and Andrew realized that this guy was managing to do all this damage while still limited to the confines of a straightjacket. God help them all if he got out of it.

The guy took another lunge, smashing himself into the bars of the door and causing Call-Me-David to take a few surprised steps back. A roaring silence fell over everyone as the sound of straining iron bars worked its way into the ambience followed by the sound of tearing seams in heavy white canvas. Silence coated the area, broken only by the sounds the chips of smashed white paint made hitting the dirty white tiles of the floor. Everyone seemed to be holding a collective breath until finally the madman spoke.

"Let me out of here!" the man in the

straightjacket growled, pressing his face against the bars. The demand was directed at Dr. Vitalis.

"Now, Gerald, you kn—"

"Don't call me that!!" Mr. Straightjacket howled, smashing himself into the bars and sending more paint chips fluttering to the floor like broken flowers as the iron bars bent further under the strain.

"Just calm down—"

"*Fuck* you and your words! I want to see my *wife*! Where is she? What have you done with her?" Mr. Straightjacket's blazing green eyes narrowed with rage and his long black hair hung in spidery disarray all across his face, deepening the already dark shadows that had settled around his eyes and beneath his prominent cheekbones. "You've already given her to *him*, haven't you?"

One of the orderlies slowly advanced on Mr. Straightjacket from behind, two needles poised and ready in each of his large hands as he drew in for the kill. And kill he just might, with two doses of what Andrew assumed was tranquilizer. Suddenly Mr.

Straightjacket was staring pure enraged insanity straight into Andrew's eyes and Andrew froze, fearing for his very life. And then it was broken, as was the stealthy orderly, but not before he had gotten both syringes emptied into his towering target.

The howl of rage was deafening and hair-raising. Mr. Straightjacket frothed at the mouth like a wild animal in the last stages of rabies, but there was no one there to shoot him. Then there was Dr. Vitalis with his award-winning bedside manner pumping yet another needle into the writhing madman. Andrew almost pitied the guy as he watched him lean more heavily against the bars, his eyes becoming glassy as they stared in front of him.

When two of the orderlies tried to get near him, Mr. Straightjacket forced himself to his feet with the speed of a killer. The seams of the straightjacket finally gave way under the increased pressure and the lunatic was free. His chalk-white skin blended with the surrounding whiteness as he lashed out at those that tried to confine him.

Andrew began to wonder if he wasn't going to die after all when Mr. Straightjacket-no-more managed to bend the bars of the door and break through the locks after one more lunge at the iron bars. The sound of ripping metal was like an explosion and Mr. Straightjacket stood there, staring like a coke-head at Dr. Vitalis, hatred plastered across his face. The doctor swallowed and the mental ward fell dead silent. Even the yells and screams of the other patients ceased abruptly as if they knew what was going on, waiting and wanting it to happen.

"Nemesis…," Dr. Vitalis began, dropping the empty syringe to the floor and holding his hands palms-out in a placating I-have-nothing-to-hide gesture as he made his way slowly and cautiously toward the freed madman.

"You son of a *bitch*!" the lunatic called Nemesis spat, "I should kill you for what you've done, but you drug me… and torment me…."

Nemesis wobbled slightly on his feet and squinted to look down at Vitalis now. He ran long white fingers through his unkempt hair and shook his head. "You are one of *us*… Why do you do this?"

"To keep you away from humanity."

Nemesis blinked at the doctor and a slow grin spread across his face. Then he laughed. "And you call *me* crazy? You *idiot*! You don't know," he paused and struggled to catch his balance, but it was a slow failure. "The Furies…." The wobble turned into a sway and Nemesis fell toward one of the barred windows, clinging to the metal reinforcing mesh on the other side of the bars to keep his balance. The scene gave Andrew the distinct impression of witnessing the fall of a Redwood tree.

"When I get out of here…," Nemesis muttered almost incoherently. He was on his hands and knees now, fighting the tranquilizers with every last ounce of strength. His breathing was labored and shallow, and he looked up at Andrew with heavy-lidded eyes.

"You never will," the doctor told his patient coldly, and swiftly, so swiftly that Andrew wondered if he had imagined it, he kicked Nemesis across the side of the head, sending the giant to the floor at last. The staff crowded around the fallen man and hastily dressed him in another straightjacket and added leg restraints to the ensemble. It took six large men to lift him onto a stretcher and return him to his padded cell. Formal dress seemed to be a mandatory element in this place, Andrew mused, his mental voice full of sarcasm. He wrinkled his nose at the thought of what might be for dinner.

"Well, Andy, I guess maybe you'll be a little bit nicer to Dav—Dr. Vitalis now. He just saved our lives."

"I guess you forgot why I'm here to begin with, Mom. Can't say I'm too thrilled." His words didn't even phase her. And now she was calling him Andy, too? He shook his head at her and sneered a dead 'Thank you' to the ever-popular doctor. Andrew wished that Nemesis guy hadn't been so doped up. He would have loved to see someone beat the living shit out of his doctor's smiling face.

During Andrew's "visit" to the mental ward—which seemed to be a hell of a lot longer than the assured "short" length of time—he saw Nemesis quite often, none of the times a particularly pleasant experience. Nemesis's room was next door to Andrew's, in fact. A detail that Dr. Immortal Love-Muffin had failed to mention when Andrew's mother was there. Every night Andrew could hear the man alternately called Nemesis(preferable) or Gerald(with much difficulty) pacing back and forth and slamming himself against the door. And then there were the fun and frequent nights that Nemesis spent screaming to be let out, that his father was in his room with him, tormenting him and telling him he had his wife. The worst part was that sometimes on those occasions, Andrew could hear a second voice in Nemesis's room. The second voice was absolutely terrifying and it took hours for Andrew to be able to get to sleep after hearing it.

This particular night was a maddening and horrifying repetition of all the others. Nemesis paced, back and forth, back and forth, and Andrew covered his head with a pillow when Nemesis started shouting. Strangely enough, the rest of the ward kept quiet when Nemesis started shouting time, as if they were sane enough to be afraid of him. At that point Andrew didn't give a rat's ass about fear. He hadn't slept in days, had started to hallucinate yesterday, and he just wanted the guy to be quiet.

"Hey, Nemesis, or whoever the hell you are at the moment: *shut up!*"

The mental ward fell silent and Andrew relaxed into his pillow. Sleep at last.

"Hey, Andrew," a deep voice growled from the darkness outside Andrew's door—or was it in the room with him? Oh, Jesus-God-in-Heaven, the guy from 417 got loose again and he was going to kill Andrew for telling him to shut up.

"Andrew...."

Shit.

"Y—yes?"

"I've killed people for less than what you just did...."

"I'm sorry, sir, but—"

"Shut up and don't interrupt, you crazy shithead!"

"Yes sir!" Andrew could feel the cold trickling of sweat running over his body and he swallowed dryly. He closed his eyes tight, expecting a blow to come from the darkness, crushing his skull and leaving the staff to wonder how the hell he'd managed to commit suicide by smashing his own head in.

"I'll tell you what will happen to you... I'm going to let you live. That will be your punishment. After I'm through with you, I'm going to let you *live*."

"Hey, look, I—"

"I said *shut up*," the voice hissed angrily, "I'm not done yet."

There was a hideously long silence as the

guard made his rounds and Andrew rushed to the door. He rushed to the small square of light coming from the small reinforced window, hands outstretched into the darkness until he finally reached that sacred square of light. When the guard passed by his room Andrew tapped at the window lightly to get the large man's attention, then motioned toward Nemesis's room and held a finger to his lips. The guard nodded bemused understanding. Andrew went on to mime Nemesis coming to attack him in the night and the guard shook his head and laughed quietly. He glanced into Nemesis's room and then moved back to Andrew. He pointed to Nemesis's room and made the motions for sleep and Andrew shook his head vehemently. The guard frowned at him, checked again, nodded, and walked away, leaving Andrew to fear the darkness alone.

Damn. Andrew pressed his shaking hands against the window and pressed his head against the door's cool surface. At least his psycho neighbor didn't know what had just taken place. Andrew shuddered to think of what could have happened to him if Nemesis found out.

"Try anything like that again and you'll find out."

Andrew spun around, mouth open in complete terror, to face into the dark room. The voice had come from behind him, he knew it. Nemesis had somehow managed to get into his room and now he was going to kill him and—

"Stop babbling, you little brat."

Andrew blinked with even more fear. This guy could read minds?! Oh, shit, was he in trouble. He could hear movement in the room with him now, coming closer, and he opened his mouth. He barely had enough time to make so much as a squeak before a large leather-gloved hand clamped over his face and pulled him back into the darkest shadows of the room. When the hands released him he could only sit in stunned silence for a moment, like a rabbit caught in a snare, and then slow coherence of his situation.

"Oh, God, please—"

"Shut up."

He could hear Nemesis circling him in the darkness and he closed his eyes in a vain attempt to will himself to wake up just in case it was a dream. There was no way this could be real. He tested the cold reality of the floor and the all-too-real presence of the psycho killer as he paced across the room, then he felt him kneel down next to him followed by the more than real sensation of wet warmth spreading across his crotch.

"Not real," Andrew whimpered.

"Wrong. Quite real," Nemesis told him, and then in a tone of barely veiled disgust, "And you've pissed yourself."

That was the last thing on Andrew's mind, the smell of his own urine faint in comparison to the more immediate threat kneeling next to him. "What are you going to do to me?"

"I'm going to cut you up and eat you for dinner, of course."

Andrew gasped and quickly realized it was a joke when he felt Nemesis smiling in the darkness. "Actually, I was just going to talk while I still can."

"Huh?"

"Tonight is your lucky night, Andy! I'm in as good a mood as I can get while locked in an asylum for the terminally insane, and since you and I have enough in common for the moment, I'm not going to kill you," Andrew felt Nemesis's breath, hot against his face as the man leaned closer, "but that isn't a promise that I won't one of these days."

"I don't get it, why me?"

"Because you and I are the most sane people in this place."

At first Andrew wasn't sure if that was another of Nemesis's little jokes, but quickly nodded in fearful agreement when he sensed Nemesis was being serious. Jesus, this guy thought he was *sane*?!

"Don't you dare think otherwise of me," Nemesis told him threateningly. No wonder they only let felt-tip pens into this place. God only knew how creative Nemesis would get with a ball-point.

"I can't stay long," the older man told Andrew suddenly, as if only a few seconds ago they had been having a friendly conversation instead of making death threats.

"So soon?" Andrew clamped a hand over his mouth, cursing his verbal reflexes of sarcasm. At least Nemesis didn't notice the slip, or was mercifully ignoring it.

"Vitalis gave me needles.... I think perhaps too many this time. I can only fight the poison for a short time before it sends me into sleep."

"Poison?" Andrew's eyes widened.

"Yes. Atropa Belladonna... or was it Valerian? I can never be sure. Lamia is the one who would know these things. She always knew her poisons and cures."

"Was Lamia your wife?"

"Yes, she *is* my wife. Never speak of her as

is she were dead."

"Is she?"

"I don't know."

Andrew heard the first hints of real fear and misery creeping into Nemesis's words. The man was in some serious denial. From the sounds of it, his wife was dead.

"She's not dead!"

Andrew swallowed his own fear back, reminding himself that Nemesis could read his mind somehow, then damning himself for not having remembered that in the first place.

"O.K.! Sorry...."

"Goodnight."

And he was gone, just like that. If he'd ever been there at all. For the first time since he had been institutionalized, Andrew began to doubt his sanity.

The next morning found Andrew feeling groggy and completely restless. He'd spent the remainder of the night trying to shake the fear that Nemesis would return and trying get relaxed enough to fall asleep even though he'd been exhausted. Now, with the dreary sun slanting through his window and the Angel of Death staring down at him from the corner of the room, Andrew just wished he was dead. His senses snapped to instant life as his eyes snapped back to where Azrael stood.

"Jesus! Do you have to that?" Andrew greeted with grouchy surprise.

"Do what?" Azrael asked innocently.

"Nevermind…. What are you doing here? Didn't think I'd see you again for a while yet." He rubbed at the aching spot on the side of his neck and winced at the pain it caused. Damn, he must have slept wrong.

"I am not here for you. I shall be needed soon, however, and decided to see how you are—or if you had changed your mind."

"Well. Thanks for caring, I'm fine… umm…. What do you mean you will be needed soon?" A slow chill of unease crept up Andrew's spine and settled between his shoulder blades while he watched Azrael watching him.

"Just as I've said," the Angel of Death replied, resting a long, thin arm against the window frame through the bars.

"Yeah, I got that, but what did you *mean* by it?"

Azrael smiled at him. "Nothing at all. I am merely carrying out my function."

Andrew sighed in frustration and turned as he heard the click of the lock on room 417's door as it opened. He opened his mouth and shut it again. What exactly would he gain from raising an alarm that Nemesis had gotten loose? Maybe his own death, and that was about it.

"Duty calls," Azrael said and moved toward the door, smiling amiably. He turned only to add, "I shall see you soon enough."

Andrew stared nervously after Azrael as he

moved out into the hallway, following behind Nemesis's looming shadow.

All told, ten people died that day at Nemesis's hands. Andrew's mother sent over their local priest, Reverend Lucien Asmodeus, to bless the dead and give confession to her son. Andrew waited in the TV room, seated next to his psychotic "new friend" as his mother liked to put it. His "new friend" was a rather doped-up, sedated to the point of near comatose version of Nemesis. Andrew still sat out of arm's reach, even though Nemesis was nearly unconscious and wearing his "dinner jacket". It was safer that way.

Nemesis's stared dulled and murky green-gray at the television in its cage, his body slumped from the tranquilizers (Andrew suspected they were using straight horse tranquilizers on him these days since it was the only thing that got him to calm down) and a thin string of pink saliva dribbling from his lower lip and onto the front of the straightjacket.

As a joke, one of the braver—or stupider—staff members with a sick sense of humor had put a smiley sticker on the front of the jacket and two nametags. The one tag read "Gerald" and the other "Nemesis". Andrew stared at the alluring and blinding tackiness of the glaring yellow smiley face and shook his head in disgust. Even the fucking workers were crazy.

"Andrew Desmond?"

He pulled his gaze from his drooling companion to see a tallish, sturdily-built death metal singer disguised as a Roman Catholic priest. Somehow Andrew didn't think this guy was what the church had had in mind for the perfect society. The man had shoulder-length wavy brown hair pulled back into a ponytail and the fiercest eyes Andrew had ever seen in a sane human being. A dark brown goatee circled the priest's strangely sensuous lips and Andrew began to wonder if maybe Rod Serling was hiding somewhere.

"Yes?" he finally managed to say after the

initial shock.

The man held a strong hand out to Andrew, "Reverend Lucien Asmodeus," he said seriously and glanced over at Nemesis. Andrew nodded as he shook hands, wondering what religion his mother had decided they should be that week. When it came to religion, his mother was fanatically a member of the Church of the Undecided. He supposed that if she were to be called anything, it would be Religious Freelancer since she was always bouncing from faith to faith. He didn't have the heart to tell her that she was going to the same church in different towns, she seemed to be so happy with her self-image as an "open-minded individual". "I'm Andrew, obviously, and this guy's Nemesis. No one knows his *real* name, if you know what I mean."

The Reverend considered this for a moment, then smiled at Andrew. "How about those vampires?"

"Excuse me?" Andrew was almost positive he hadn't heard this guy correctly, either that or the drugs they had him on were finally starting to kick in. Whatever it was, it gave him the distinct impression that he was having an out-of-mind experience.

"The vampires. They started fighting with the normal mortals again."

The Reverend said it like he wasn't a member of the "normal mortals". Andrew nodded and smiled politely, if somewhat fearfully, at the holy man and came to a decision. His mother should have been the one in the asylum, not him.

"I started that war," Nemesis mumbled suddenly. Reverend Asmodeus stared in something bordering on rapture at the freak in the straightjacket and Andrew tried to move as far away from the both of them as possible without looking like he was doing just that. The Reverend didn't seem to notice Andrew's retreat, he was too intent on Nemesis.

"How could you have started that war from here?"

The Reverend was making himself right at

home in the TV room. He sat across from Nemesis as if they were old friends. Nemesis stared at the priest in blurred interest and concentrated on what he wanted to say.

"I wasn't always in here," Nemesis muttered, trying to focus on the Reverend, "I was married, and we were so happy…. They took her from me…. and no one will listen to me!" He looked at the holy man in bleary-eyed desperation and Reverend Asmodeus nodded sympathetically.

"Have faith in *yourself* and you'll come out alright. Your name is Nemesis?"

Nemesis nodded in slow motion.

"Nemesis, I've heard of you. I admire you. Always remember that no one can take away your freedom, not even God if He existed, which He doesn't."

Andrew looked up sharply. What kind of priest *was* this? Total shocked confusion was all he could feel at the moment, along with a growing uneasiness.

"Yes He does." Nemesis sighed. "I met him."

"You *met* God?" The Reverend leaned closer to Nemesis, a look of keen interest stamped over his features like graffiti. Nemesis nodded and tried to wipe away the drool on his chin.

"He was nice enough, but He wouldn't help me or my wife all that much, but my wife knew Him better than I did," Nemesis finished with a yawn. That was the sign that he wanted to be left alone so he could take a nap, but Reverend Asmodeus was on a mission.

"That is exactly my point! God is never around when you need Him! The *aliens* are here more often than He is. Which brings me to my next question: Have you ever met the Devil?"

Nemesis tried to glare and only pulled off a bored expression. "You mean my father?"

The comment was meant to end the conversation in fearful awe, but the Reverend crusaded bravely onward. He didn't realize that

Nemesis was being serious, he just assumed he had a complex because he was crazy.

"Have you considered Satanism as religious possibility?"

Just when Andrew thought his eyebrows couldn't go any higher. A priest on a crusade to promote Satanism?

"Leave me alone."

"Or maybe Devil-worship? They're not the same, you know. One—"

"Shut up and leave me alone," Nemesis growled. The room activity ceased and silence fell as the other patients turned to stare at those that would provoke Nemesis. Andrew shifted uncomfortably and scratched at the stitches on his wrists. He cleared his throat, drawing the Reverend's angry stared challenge away from Nemesis and his increasingly more alert gaze.

"Reverend Asmodeus, do you remember all those people that died today?"

"Yes, of course."

Andrew nodded toward Nemesis, "Meet the man responsible."

"I see. Well, Nemesis, the war and now this? Why not change religions now before the Christians have you burning in Hell?"

Nemesis turned his cold, glittering green stare onto the priest and a deep frown curled the corners of his mouth. "Didn't I ask you very nicely to be quiet?" There was no murkiness left in that look. Andrew had learned to recognize the color changes in Nemesis's eyes like a broken mood ring. Green meant psychotic, gray meant sedated. There wasn't even a hint of gray left in the eyes now.

Andrew grabbed Reverend Asmodeus by the arm and led him out of the TV room as quickly as possible.

"Just what the hell are you doing, kid?"

"Saving your life. When he gets like that, trust me, you don't want to piss him off, O.K.?"

Reverend Asmodeus frowned and glanced back into the TV room as Nemesis finished getting to his feet, wobbling in near seven feet. The Reverend blinked and quickly averted his eyes, following Andrew down the hallway. "Jesus. He's a hell of a lot taller in person…. Where are we going?"

Andrew looked up at him and smirked at the expression on the Reverend's face. He'd seen it many times before, usually as a result of the first meeting with Nemesis. Now the expression rested over Reverend Asmodeus's face like a veil.

"We'll go back to my room…. Then you can tell me why my mother thinks I need spiritual guidance from a Satanic Priest."

The Reverend seemed to smile at that. "Shows that much, huh?"

"Like a beacon, guy."

Andrew nearly jumped out of his skin at the peal of maniacal laughter that burst from the man in priest's clothing. He hit into the doorframe as he entered the room, smacking his knee against the edge of the frame.

"Damn!"

"You okay?"

"Yeah," Andrew mumbled angrily while rubbing his knee. He looked up to see Azrael grinning and giving him a sarcastic thumbs-up and then he was gone. Andrew started and then shook his head while hopping over to the bed. "I just miscalculated where the door was is all." He motioned for the Reverend to take a seat and they regarded each other silently for a moment.

"So…," Andrew began.

"So," the Reverend said and nodded.

"Why did my mother send you?"

"She felt you lacked religious diversity, and your recent… occurrence," the unholy man motioned to Andrew's stitched wrists, "only made her more sure of your lack of self confidence. In Satanism suicide is the ultimate sin because it is the destruction of the most important thing: you. She's an interesting woman, your mother."

"Yeah, tell me about it. It took a suicide attempt for me to learn even this much about her.... Hey, listen, this whole bit," Andrew motioned at his wrists with the impatient familiarity of someone with an obvious visible defect who had to constantly explain it to people that stared enough to be obvious about it, "it wasn't because I had low self-esteem," he laughed at the thought, then, "Leave it to my mother to misinterpret everything I do. At first she thought I tried to off myself because of her, then my ex-girlfriend thought I did it because I caught her and my best friend together—Jesus H.! Women, huh? I hate them sometimes."

"I don't know about all that. I actually enjoy women immensely," the Reverend said with a lewd smile, his eyes far away in a distant erotic memory.

"For dinner, right?" Andrew smiled only half-sarcastically. He could easily picture this guy eating human flesh and washing it down with blood. The Reverend seemed to read his intent and his smile widened.

"Sometimes that, too."

They fell into an awkward silence, Andrew looking around while the Reverend stared at him fixedly. Andrew ran a hand through his barely brushed hair and recognized the gesture as a habit that Nemesis displayed often. He quickly dropped his hand to his lap and grasped it with the other one.

"Yeah, well…," he said, finally shattering the unnerving silence, "I gotta go to dinner soon, and Dr. Vitalis usually comes to check on me before then, so I should be getting ready and—"

"Why *did* you do it?"

"What?"

"Why did you try to kill yourself?"

Andrew stared at the priest for a moment of silence, then shrugged. "I got bored…."

"So you try to *kill* yourself?"

"No! …No. That came out wrong. I guess what I'm trying to say is that I got bored with life.

Let's face it, I'm going nowhere in life anyway. Not with my mother the way she is, you know? So what else do I have to look forward to? A happy marriage? Yeah, right. Women destroy you one way or another, and forget being gay. Even if I was that way, my mother would get a permanent complex over it. So I can't have sex, can't get money in the area I'm in, can't get away from home without guilt—hell, if I got to be rich and famous Mom would think I was trying to leave her to be with my 'decadent' friends. No matter what, I lose!" Andrew paced the small white room and grasped the bars on his window, staring out at the darkening landscape. He turned to look at the priest again. *"Now* do you see?" He pulled an agitated hand through his hair and suddenly caught himself. Pacing, talking to himself, and now pulling his hand through his hair. He was turning into Nemesis. Jesus.

The Reverend Lucien Asmodeus, Death Metal singer and Satanic Priest, nodded gravely. Without saying anything, he reached into the black backpack he'd brought with him, taking out a pair of shoelaces, a razorblade, and a bottle of prescription tranquilizers.

"A gun would be too obvious," the Reverend finally said after placing the instruments of destruction on the table. Andrew stared from the table to the priest, then back to the table in numb shock.

"You… *want* me to kill myself?" he asked incredulously.

"I didn't say that. I believe in freedom of choice and in natural selection to a degree. If you're malfunctioning that badly, it's obvious you at least need the right to choose." The Reverend reached into his backpack before zipping it and held up a copy of The Satanic Bible in a final wave. "May your death be quick and painless. Go in peace."

Andrew stared at the departing priest, his mind only half-registering that the man was going in the opposite direction of the exit. He fell heavily into the chair and let his gaze wander over his potential demise spread out before him like a poker hand. He stayed like that for a long time, part of him expecting Azrael to make an appearance, but he didn't. Andrew only moved when the guard came to call them for dinner and Andrew shoved his new treasure under the mattress.

That night he couldn't sleep. He lay in his bed with his hands folded behind his head, staring up at the ceiling. He could feel the bulges of the objects he's hidden and he thought back to the night he had opened his veins in the bath, the way the water turned red in clouds. It looked almost like he had rinsed out paintbrushes with red paint on them.

Andrew turned his head, slowly drawn out of his morbid musings by the muffled sound of voices from next door. From Nemesis's room. A shiver crept up his spine and settled over his heart when he recognized the voice of the Reverend Asmodeus.

Quietly, Andrew got to his feet, feeling the reality of the cold tiles of the floor on his bare feet as he padded over to the far wall. Normally he wasn't an eavesdropper, but one word had caught his attention: vampire. Andrew pressed his ear to the wall and held his breath without even making a conscious effort to do so. The moon slanted through the window, leaving barred shadows stretching across the pale white light on the floor. Something about the way the moonlight slanted over the floor made Andrew think of Halloween and October, of falling leaves and the scent of smoke in the air. It had to be getting close to that time of year, he mused. And then the certainty that they weren't going to let him out of there settled over his heart. They were going to keep him locked away in this creepy place because Dr. Vitalis was trying to move in on his mother. Damn that bastard. He could tell them whatever he wanted to, too, because he was the doctor and Andrew was just a crazy mental patient who'd tried to off himself. His mother never came to visit him anymore, she stayed for a few minutes and then left with the doctor. No one would ever know he was there….

Andrew shut his eyes and tried to block the

bad thoughts as he pressed his ear more tightly to the wall. He could hear the Reverend clearly now, and again the shiver ran up his spine.

"I know all about it, and I want to be a part of it. Make me like you."

"You have no idea what you're asking—"

"Yes, dammit, I *do*! I know *exactly* what I'm asking! …Do this for me and I'll go and tell the others where you are, what they've done to you."

Andrew could hear heavy pacing in the silence. Nemesis. Whatever Asmodeus was trying to offer or get, Nemesis was seriously considering it. Finally, after a moment of silence, the pacing stopped and Nemesis's voice came through the wall, deep and resonating.

"Alright. I'll do it… not because I like you, I don't. I do it only because I need you, and I want revenge."

"You won't regret it," Asmodeus said, voice choked with emotion and Andrew could hear the manic grin that covered the man's mouth.

"If I do, you won't live long enough to figure it out," Nemesis said, and now he sounded like he was smiling, too. Andrew wondered what the hell was going on over there.

"Give me your wrist."

Andrew heard a gasp and groan, followed by the sound of deadweight hitting the floor.

"Your turn," Nemesis breathed, "Drink. Hurry."

Then a groan so deep and animalistic it could only have come from Nemesis's throat, and the night was still once more.

"Hurry up and leave while there's time...."

The almost silent click of 417's door opening and closing was followed by the dark shape of the Reverend slipping down the corridor. When the man was out of earshot Andrew heard Nemesis laughing in the darkness.

"And before you die," Nemesis finished.

Andrew had an idea of just what was going on now, and he'd almost made up his mind on what he wanted to do with his life. He wanted to get rid of it. Maybe. He would talk it over with Nemesis and figure it all out.

As he was about to knock on the wall he heard the main gate open and shut, and then footsteps hurrying angrily past his door. Vitalis. Shit. Andrew had been wrong about him, this guy was perfect for his mother. They both had impeccable timing. The doorlatch on 417 clicked open and shut again, and now he heard Vitalis pacing in Nemesis's room.

"Just what the *hell* did you think you were doing, Gerald?"

"Nemesis."

"What?!" the doctor hissed.

"My name is *Nemesis*, **not** Gerald."

Andrew realized he was holding his breath and didn't give a rat's ass. When Nemesis used that deep, threatening tone, it meant someone was going to die. He was glad Vitalis was the one in 417 and he smiled. The final test of the immortal Love-Muffin's mortality was at hand and this time the fight was going to be good. Doctor Love must have had a date, because he sure as hell hadn't been around to give Nemesis his "medication". Andrew's smile widened. Had there been anyone there to witness the way he was crouched and grinning like a madman, they would have thrown him into a straightjacket just on principle.

He heard the creek of the bed as Nemesis's weight left the mattress. The silence crashed around the mental ward and Andrew felt the air charging with some kind of current. He squinted at his arms in the cold darkness and ran a hand over the skin on his forearms, feeling the goosebumps there, and something else. Something strange. All of the hair on his arms was standing on end. He reached a hand up to his head, not surprised to find the hair there also trying to pull out at the roots. And the air seemed to be heating up.

"Nemesis, don't do this. They'll kill you if

you do this."

The smile in Nemesis's words was more than apparent, "Maybe… but how will they ever know if they don't find your body?"

Now Dr. Vitalis was stumbling backwards, toward the door, as the air around them became supercharged.

"You were warned."

"No! Wait!"

Andrew heard a noise that could only be electricity zapping through the air next door. It sounded a lot like the sound effects they used to use to enhance the Jacob's Ladders in the old black and white movies with mad scientists.

"What about your wife?"

"What about her?" the electricity in the air made Andrew want to scream, and he almost did when he felt a small but painful zap in the back of his mouth as the fillings in his teeth transferred the current between his upper and lower molars. It felt like he had bitten into a ball of aluminum foil and started chewing.

"I know where she is," Vitalis said smugly, the voice of a poker player trying to bluff.

"Bullshit," Andrew whispered and clamped a hand over his mouth.

"Bullshit," Nemesis said almost at the same time and Andrew nearly burst out laughing.

"I mean it!" Vitalis gasped as the electric level in the air next door let off an audible *zap!* that must have connected with the doctor's precious person. Andrew felt like laughing again.

"Then where is she?"

Vitalis's breath caught in an audible choke when Nemesis called his bluff. "N-now, hold on ....
Why don't I just give you your medication first?" he tried hopefully. Andrew shook his head in amused disbelief. Nemesis was crazy, not stupid. This suggestion was met by the sound of a quick slap and the clink of plastic and metal hitting the floor.

"Time for you to take some, Vitalis," Nemesis laughed darkly.

"No! OW! Dammit, Nemesis, I've only tried to help you."

"You've tried to help the human race escape me while profiting from it. You're one of the Undead, but you aren't one of my kind. You're much too young to remember the old days and the old ways. But you're not too young to know that I am a god.... Now tell me where Lamia is before the sedative kicks in, will you?"

"I don't know where she is."

"Liar."

Andrew heard the latch on 417 open once more and marveled at the fact that none of the guards had come running at all the noise. He saw two shadows move past his door and then he was up and moving toward the doorway. He wasn't aware of what he was going to do until he called out to Nemesis as he and the doctor moved down the hall.

"Nemesis."

The larger shadow turned, the moonlight slanting barred shadows over its face and igniting the blaze of psychosis in its green stare. No murkiness in those eyes anymore. Now they all but glowed a bright emerald green. Andrew felt the words catch in his throat as his eyes followed Nemesis's arms up to Dr. Vitalis's neck. One of Nemesis's large hands held the doctor by the back of the neck at the base of his skull while the other held the emptied syringe in the doctor's throat. It took Andrew a second to understand that Nemesis meant to pump air into the sedated man's bloodstream and kill him quickly and quietly if need be. Andrew had to smile at Nemesis's ingenuity.

"I want to go with you."

Nemesis arched one thin black eyebrow in a working of facial muscles Andrew had never been able to master and a grin spread across the man's wide, harsh lips. "Do you now? Well then, come on. We haven't got all night." Easy as that. Andrew rushed to catch up.

When they reached the guards' station Andrew discovered why none of the men had noticed what was going on. They were all asleep. Nemesis walked forward, past the sleeping guards, and tried the door with its bent bars only to find it locked. With a growl and a grinding of metal on metal he pushed the door wide, snapping the lock in two, and dragging Dr. Vitalis by the hair as they made their way into the darkness, in the opposite direction of escape.

"Hey, Nemesis? The exit's over that way," Andrew whispered, confused.

"I know."

"So then… why go this way?"

Nemesis turned to face him, eyes blazing in the cold light of the moon. The moment seemed to stretch as Dr. Vitalis suddenly pushed Nemesis into the metal bars of the windows hard enough to bend them. He only made it a few yards back toward the main part of the mental ward before Nemesis tackled him and drove the needle back into the doctor's neck. He pinned the doctor with his body and turned his full attention back to Andrew.

"If you make so much as a fucking WHEEZE, I'm going to do this to *you*," Nemesis snarled, motioning to Dr. Vitalis, "And I don't think you'll survive half as well as he will."

Andrew's terrified gaze shifted from Nemesis's psychotic eyes, his face a mask of murder, to the prone form of the doctor. The man's eyes stared up at him, glazed over from the sedative intended for Nemesis, and his throat convulsed for a moment and then he whispered, "Andy…, get help."

Andrew flinched as Nemesis drove the needle into the man's neck until the plastic of the syringe hit against the skin.

"Shut UP!" Nemesis screamed and then he looked back at Andrew. "You move toward that direction and I'll kill you, too. Got it?"

Andrew stared at the gruesome scene, unable to speak and Nemesis moved as if to catch him.

Andrew cried out and jumped away from him, and Nemesis asked again, stressing every word with a push of the needle. "Do you understand?"

Andrew nodded dumbly, his jaw hanging open as he watched the twisted fucking of the needle into his doctor's neck. This wasn't going the way he'd planned it at all, and he glanced longingly over his shoulder and wished he'd stayed in bed. There was no turning back now, he was trapped in this whole mess and most likely he'd end up as an accomplice to murder. With a soft sigh of fearful resignation and self-preservation, he followed Nemesis down the corridor and into the even creepier areas of the mental ward.

They were going into the old West Wing. It had been closed down for quite some time, long before Andrew's mother's time, even. He'd only ever heard rumors in school about it, mostly stories of hauntings, but ghost stories told in the light of day don't carry any weight until they're thought of again during the night... or if the person happens to be walking through the scene of the story with a certified psycho who was a vampire. A real one.

Andrew looked at his darkening surroundings with a shudder of unease. The paint peeled down the walls in crackling leaded flypaper strips and there were dark water stains running adjacent to the unused water pipes all along the corridors. The linoleum tiles of the floor had pulled up and buckled from repeated water damage over the decades of abandonment and the air was chilly and smelled like an old basement even in the wake of the hot late-summer night.

There were a large number of rooms lining the hallway, their doors ajar and clinging to the rusted hinges, and Andrew expected to see any number of patients-past peeking around the doorway and watching them walk by, but the only occupants left in the deserted wing were a very few large rats that stood on their hind legs, sniffing at the trio as they moved near them. They were eerily bold as they moved toward their legs, squeaking as if with menacing laughter like some kind of rodent street gang.

One of the rats intercepted Nemesis and he kicked it with such savage force that its bones could be heard cracking when it hit the wall. The others seemed to take the hint and moved away quickly and Nemesis shuddered. "I *hate* rats," he growled, and Andrew thought he could almost hear another voice tangled within Nemesis's, and that voice didn't hate the rats, it was *terrified* of them. Nemesis's eyes flickered from their usual green ice to gray steel in the moonlight as he stared back at Andrew, and they were almost sane. They stared with compassion at Andrew briefly, and then they were green once more as Nemesis dragged the doctor onward into the gloomy darkness. Andrew shivered in the chilled air of the dilapidated corridor of the fourth floor's unused, unmentioned West Wing and hurried to catch up with Nemesis.

As they went on, Andrew glanced back repeatedly, every nerve in his body tingling with fear. He was sure that he had heard the high-pitched cackle of a lunatic echoing at him from out of one of the empty rooms, and as they moved further into the darkness he became even more sure that he caught sight of someone ducking into the many lurking shadows surrounding them. He would have sighed with relief when they finally reached their destination, except that it was even worse than the journey.

They entered some type of operating room with all the fixings for a good old-fashioned shock treatment session and lobotomy chaser. The whole room was lit from above, by a scummed-over skylight, with the moon shining through the white haze, bathing the faded hospital green and white peeling-paint walls in a ghastly glow.

Nemesis heaved the doctor onto an ancient, rusted stretcher that took up the middle of the room. He quickly fastened the brittle leather cuffs around the man's wrists and ankles, then stepped back to admire his work while Dr. Vitalis stared up at him with large, frightened eyes. Nemesis leaned over him, and with a sadistic smile he pushed the plunger of the syringe in, sending air straight into the doctor's bloodstream.

"No!" both Andrew and Dr. Vitalis cried out simultaneously. The word echoed off the walls and slammed back at them and Andrew cringed. Nemesis was prepared, as always, and quickly pulled the needle from the doctor's vein and shoved it into the man's vocal chords so that he wouldn't be able to make any more noise when the real pain hit in mere seconds.

Dr. Vitalis arched completely off the stretcher as the pain lanced through the sedatives and brought him screaming silently back into reality. He stared with a mingling of horror and hate at Nemesis and the ancient god smiled down at him as he picked up the equipment formerly used to perform shock treatment.

"Let the fun begin," Nemesis said, and his smile widened.

Andrew watched in amazement as Nemesis charged the long-dead equipment with his bare hands. Sparks of electricity leapt from the rotted ends of the crescent-shaped conductors, lighting the room with an eerie, pale blue glow. Nemesis fitted the open end of the crescent over Dr. Vitalis's head until the two rotted, sparking ends met the man's temples. Nemesis stared at Vitalis for a moment, thoughtfully tapping his lower lip with one long, slender white index finger. "I'm forgetting something…," he said from far away. He quickly brightened. "I forgot to plug it in!" He wobbled the shock equipment on the doctor's head and laughed. "Not that it matters, right?"

Nemesis looked around the room as if searching for a final ingredient to a cake recipe. He found it moldering in a corner near the stretcher and moved to place it in his former doctor's mouth.

Don't you dare, Vitalis mouthed and Nemesis stuck his hand into the man's mouth, prying the lower jaw forcefully away from the upper set of straight, even white teeth and pushing the blackened wooden thing resembling a dog's old chew-toy in between the doctor's spread jaws. When Vitalis tried to spit it out, Nemesis held his hand over his mouth and searched through the doctor's coat pockets, finally pulling out a roll of medical tape. With a smile, and while humming a familiar tune that Andrew recognized as a song by the Eurythmics, "Sweet Dreams", Nemesis taped the mouthpiece in, wrapping Dr. Vitalis's head several times with the medical tape. Almost as an afterthought, he slapped a strip across the doctor's eyelids and eyebrows, taping his eyes open. Andrew felt sick and dizzy, and he bumped against an old cart piled high with rusted instruments on his way toward the wall. He wanted to wake up in his nice, warm, government-issue bed and forget that this whole terrible nightmare had ever taken place.

Nemesis made minor adjustments on his victim, then in a dramatic movement that would haunt Andrew for a long time, he violently pulled the needle out of the doctor's throat with the words, "Sound check, Vitalis. Go ahead and make some noise for me."

Dr. Vitalis groaned as his eyes watered from the taped stare. His gray eyes searched the room, artificially hectic, and locked onto Andrew as he tried to inconspicuously fade into the wall. Andrew flinched at the naked fear in the huge exposed eyes and sighed at the simultaneous plea in them.

"Nemesis? Hey, man, this isn't right. It's—" Andrew's words died in his throat when Nemesis turned his crazed, bright green stare onto him. "It's *revenge*," Nemesis smiled. Andrew stared into those green eyes and then down to the sharp, elongated eye teeth poking out of Nemesis's smile. "Revenge?" he asked weakly.

"Yes…. Before you got here with your luscious tidbit of a mother to distract him, our friend here was quite the sadist. Put me to shame…," the madman's eyes became distant as he looked down at his victim, "He'd fill his nights up by doing *this* to *me* instead of going out and sucking your mother dry while they fucked."

Andrew felt the bile burning the back of his throat, hoping against hope that Nemesis was lying, but all it took was one look at Dr. Vitalis to see the guilt in the man's taped eyes. "Oh, Jesus… you really *are* a vampire… and you've been doing… *that* to my mother?"

The doctor averted his eyes and groaned. Andrew had been his only hope of escape.

"And you've been sucking my mother's blood?"

When Vitalis wouldn't look at Andrew, Nemesis took the opportunity to twist the screw he'd planted. "David here hides behind his doctor's title, using his patients up until they die… or until he ships them off to the mental ward. After all, there's no such thing as a vampire, right, Doc?" Nemesis's eyes blazed as he pulled the doctor's head by the hair into a sickening semblance of a nod. "Motherfucker, you pulled the same shit with me… told me I was crazy and that I wasn't a vampire. The whole time you were one of us! Weren't you?!" Again the forced nod. "That's what I thought."

Nemesis pushed the doctor's head back onto the table, giving a rough pull on the man's hair. "I'm not flattered that you stole my blood, either, Vitalis… and I am definitely not amused with my imprisonment here…. Are you ready to cooperate with me now?"

Dr. Vitalis nodded, his eyes huge, black, and vast in the darkness.

"Good," Nemesis purred, "Tell me where my wife is."

The doctor groaned against the gag and Nemesis's smile widened to the point that Andrew could see the man's back teeth.

"Wrong answer."

Andrew felt sick again as the air in the room charged up. Nemesis's hands glowed with electricity as he wrapped them around the metal crescent encircling the doctor's head, and then an audible *ZAP!* as the charge reached its crescendo. The man writhed in agony on the stretcher, back arched at an uncomfortably impossible angle, his fingers and legs twitching spastically even after Nemesis stopped the current.

Tears streamed down the doctor's face and his eyes stared wildly up at Nemesis. His fingers continued to twitch and the pungent smell of burning hair began to filter into the room as Andrew backed toward the doorway. He'd had enough and hoped Nemesis would either let him go or kill him quickly, anything as long as he didn't have to sit through this demonstration in sadism.

"Just where the hell do you think *you're* going?"

Andrew froze at the doorway and his eyes rolled wildly toward Nemesis. His mouth worked in mute fear as his finger pointed toward the hallway outside the door.

"You'd like to think that, wouldn't you. What do *you* say about it, DOCTOR? Is he well enough to be discharged?"

ZAP!

"IS HE?"

ZAP!

"Damn you, you sonofaBITCH, answer me! I said *is he healed*?!"

ZAAAP!!

"Oh JesusGodinHeaven STOP IT! You're killing him!"

Both Nemesis and David turned to stare at Andrew as he slid down the wall with his arms covering his head. "Stop it," he begged, his voice small and ragged with sobs.

Nemesis started to laugh at him. "You just don't get it, do you, maggot? He's *immortal*. I could do this from now to eternity and he won't die… at least I don't *think* he will. Hell, I'll just have to find out."

Andrew curled into a fetal position as another charge ran through his doctor's brain. He could smell the mildew of the floortiles and if he looked hard enough he could see the dust, anything to take him away from the horrid scene as jolt after jolt lit the room and filled the air with gagged screams and the scent of burning fabric and flesh.

"Nemesis, that's enough."

All eyes turned to the silhouette in the doorway, staring in disbelief. Andrew had assumed she'd be a little taller, but the figure was definitely nice.

"Lamia," Nemesis breathed. His hands released the metal crescent and he wiped them off on his clothes quickly before folding them under his arms guiltily.

The figure was then obscured by another, larger shadow. It was the Reverend Asmodeus.

"You're lucky this guy found me when he did, David," Lamia said, motioning to the Reverend. "I wouldn't like to put my immortality to Nemesis's tests," she laughed and shook her head as she came into the light, as if nothing was really seriously wrong with the picture before her, then, "Let him go, Nemesis. It's over."

Nemesis only stared at his wife and Andrew suddenly felt bad for the guy. As wild and out-of-control as Nemesis was, if Lamia had said jump, he'd ask how high and probably die trying to pull the stars from the sky for her.

"No probablies about it," Nemesis said with determination. Without taking his eyes off his wife, he waved a hand in the direction of the doctor and the man was free.

As Lamia was illuminated by the dim light her skin seemed to glow a pale blue and her eyes sparkled darkly, a small feline smile curling the corners of her mouth. Andrew felt his own gasp, but didn't remember having taken a breath since Lamia walked into the room. It didn't matter. Lamia was worth it. Her large dark eyes glanced to him briefly as she walked by and he felt his heart rip when she smiled at him. He blinked and she was gone, moving toward Nemesis, and he wanted to stop her, to warn her that Nemesis could be harmful or fatal to her if she let him swallow her. One look to Nemesis kept his mouth shut. The man was staring straight into his eyes with a look that stated in a silent, threatening manner that if Andrew even tried what he was thinking, he'd die painfully.

"Ready to go home, sweetie?" Lamia grinned as she jumped and hugged Nemesis around the neck.

He had to practically bend in half so she could even reach and Andrew found himself smiling. In a strange way, it was very touching.

"God, yes," Nemesis sighed into her hair as he lifted her into his arms.

"You can't leave," Dr. Vitalis suddenly broke in. "He's crazy! He'll start the war again!"

"Too late," Lamia and the Reverend smirked.

"Maybe this time things will end on a better note," Lamia sighed as she put a hand onto a place near her heart, "and I won't be put out of action again."

They began to move toward the door and Andrew was surprised to hear himself speak.

"Wait."

Nemesis and Lamia turned and Andrew felt his heart ripping again when Lamia's eyes met his. "Are you sure you want me to do that, Andrew?" she asked him.

He blushed and looked away only to see Azrael nod to him from a dark corner. Lamia followed his gaze and grinned.

"Long time, no see, Az."

"The same can be said to you, madame," the Angel of Death smiled to Lamia. He moved effortlessly across the room and grasped Lamia's hand, briefly kissing it. No one missed the look of jealous hate that Nemesis gave the angel.

"Don't you have someplace to be—like where people are dying?" Nemesis asked quietly. Azrael smiled up at him, silver eyes gleaming equal hate.

"Indeed, sir. And what better place than a hospital? At the moment, however, my place and job are both here."

"I don't understand," David began weakly, then froze in suspicious fear, "I'm—"

Azrael's impatient shake of the head and Lamia's regretful glance to Andrew silenced the doctor.

"It's me, not you, Dr. Vitalis. Take good care of my mother for me, you know, kind of explain things to her for me... O.K.?"

"Are you positive about this?" Lamia asked him gently. Andrew turned to stare at her and he wondered what it would be like to kiss her, to wake up next to her in the mornings—only there wouldn't *be* any mornings, not with her, not ever again. He nodded slowly and moved in front of her, then got down on is knees.

"Good thinking, kiddo." She leaned in close to him and whispered in his ear, "You can still change your mind. Once it's done there's no going back. You understand?"

Andrew nodded and swallowed the lump of fear burning in his throat. When Lamia put her arms around him, her small hands cupping his face and turning his head to one side, he began to panic.

"Shhh…," she whispered in his ear. "Are you sure? Do you understand what will happen to you, what I am?"

"I understand," Andrew told her thickly. She kissed away his tears and he felt like he would die… but then again, that was the point, wasn't it? He stared into her beautiful eyes as she smoothed back his hair and he felt himself becoming lighter, far away.

The pain was exquisite. It ran hot and fiery from his neck and she drank the pain away, holding him as he sank to the floor. Then there was Azrael, pulling him away from his body.

"This is a first for me, Andrew," the angel smiled at him. "First you try to end your life, and again you take your life in your own hands. Come."

Azrael led him back to his body and set him down in it. There was an almost audible click as he reconnected and sat up. Everything was so different now. He glanced over to Azrael and could finally *see* the angel as he was. A dark type of anti-light blazed around him and hurt Andrew's new and chnging eyes. A pair of raven-black wings stretched gracefully from Azrael's upper back and now he was naked, his white skin like alabaster in contrast to the wings. He had no body hair, and his limbs were long and slender, almost tapering. Andrew gasped in surprise at the true beauty of the angel, and then he saw Lamia. He knew in that instant exactly why Nemesis had willingly enslaved himself to her. He could still see her outer beauty, but now he could also see her inner beauty—her soul, whatever it might be called, and it was incredible. It was like being able to see what love looked like. Nemesis was almost the exact opposite. He embodied vengeance and power. Beauty and the Beast to an extent, and they balanced each other out nicely.

Azrael spoke to him again, and now Andrew could hear the singing of angels. "First you try to die, now you become one of the Undead," the angel shook his head and smiled, "I will never understand the workings of the human mind. Good luck with your new life, Andrew Desmond."

Andrew nodded and Azrael was gone. He looked to Lamia and she held out a hand, helping him to his feet.

"Will it always be like this?" he asked her, then he looked to Nemesis. "Will I always feel this way?"

Lamia smiled at him and shrugged. "You get used to it, I guess."

"But will it fade? Will everything become less beautiful than it is now? Will my life ever be ordinary again?"

She grinned at him, a wide, all-teeth grin, and laughed. "Hon, for me, life has never been 'ordinary'... and as for the beauty part, well, that all depends on your mood from day to day, right?"

"Yeah, I guess it does... So... what happens now?"

He stared at her and Nemesis placed a

protective hand on her shoulder. Andrew ignored the gesture as Lamia shrugged. "Now we're going back to New York. You're welcome to join us if you want."

Andrew nodded and glared over at Dr. Vitalis. "There's nothing left for me here anymore. Just promise me one thing, Doctor."

Dr. Vitalis looked at him wearily and sighed. "What's that?"

"That if you make my mother a vampire, which I'm sure you will, promise me that you'll only let her visit me once a decade. O.K.?"

The doctor smiled wryly and nodded.

"Good." Andrew looked to Lamia and gave a short nod. "I'm all set, let's go."

Andrew Desmond followed Lamia out into the night, accompanied by a Satanic Priest and a minor deity from a time so long ago that no one really remembered it anymore. He stared up into the night, letting the acid rain into his upturned eyes and smiled. At that point only God knew what the future would bring, and as usual, He wasn't talking.

THE LAST SUPPER

By

Suzi M

He watched as the blood ran down his
fingers, mingling with the paleness of his skin.
Lovely crimson splashes fell onto the worn planks of
the floor. He smiled down at his latest victim as her
own blood dripped into her staring lifeless eyes,
creating red tears that streamed down her face and

into her blood-blond hair.

"Thank you," he breathed as he held his hand aloft, watching as the last spasms echoed through the girl's dying heart. "Thank you so very much...." He brought her heart to his lips and kissed it lovingly, sucking the rest of her life from it.

The sounds of violence still rang out like machinegun-fire in the street below his window, and he moved near the broken glass to get a better view of the carnage in the streets. The Big Apple was bleeding; New York City was in ruins, and he loved it that way.

"Die, you fuckers!" he howled into the clawing night and flung the drained heart out into the throng of rioters beneath his window. By morning either the dogs or one of the undead would have eaten it off the street. "All of you can go to hell... die die DIE!" He became more agitated with his excitement and the thrill of fresh murder on his hands as he danced across the worn floor of the old factory he called home now. His footsteps pounded like a drumbeat across the walls and echoed back at him, providing accompaniment to his shouted ranting. The rhythm quickened with his screaming heart, and he felt relief again, relief from the empty void in his soul. Relief from the voices in his head.

He was whole once again, his mind was his. He was almost sane. The screams outside were dying away with the owner of the agony. A new sound caught his attention and he quickly sidestepped across the room to where the girl's body lay. He threw a sheet stained with the blood of the previous donors to his sanity-shrine over the girl and leapt into an armchair. Then he pretended to read. □

"Scott? Are you up here?"

He grimaced at the annoying whiney quality his wife's voice had acquired over the years. It was all he could do to not sacrifice her to the demons in his head.

"Yes, honey. I'm in here."

"Are you alright? I heard someone yelling."

His wife's haggard features came into view as she

walked into the puddle of a streetlamp's light. The sodium glow did nothing to hide the circles under her eyes. It only made them worse. But that was understandable, neither one of them had slept in over a week now, and he was starting to live the nightmares he would have been having.

"I was… singing." He smiled up at her tired features, remembering a time when he still loved her.

"I'm trying to sleep," she said flatly.

It was her retort for everything these days, and he hated her more every time she used it. She shuffled out of the room and he wanted to scream at her to pick up her goddam feet when she walked, but it would have been no use. She would have used her clever retort of being tired again, and he wasn't sure he'd be able to hold back the murderer inside him one more time. She paused at the girl's covered body and turned back to look at him. He had to bite his lips to hold back the snarl.

"What's that?" Accusing him of murder.

"Becky, don't worry about it, okay?" Daring

her to turn him in.

She stared at him for a long moment and he became uncomfortable.

"Look, I was working on something. A sculpture."

"Well, keep it down. I'm trying to sleep."

And that was all she said. He waited until he didn't hear the shuffle of her ratty pink bunny slippers on the hardwood floor before venturing to pull the cover from his "sculpture". It was time to start carving.

"Tell me how much you wanted it, you bitch," he whispered lovingly into her ear.

The girl's eyes stared into his, but all he saw there was that she hadn't wanted what he'd had to give. He slapped her face, but it was no use. There was no longer a response. It was time to create more artwork.

He carved across her bare smooth stomach, spilling her intestines onto the floor in one smooth waterfall motion. He stared at the girl's insides, fascinated by the color and sickened by the stench. Now all he had to do was let her dry and then the fun could begin.

He dragged her body to a small closet and hung her up next to a guy he had killed a month before. They made a cute couple.

"Sorry to break up the party, kids, but it's time for you to come down, my friend." He reached up and unhooked the mummified remains of the young guy from the meathook and threw them onto the floor. He checked the other bodies to see if they were done yet and found two more to add to the pile.

He looked up at his latest addition and smiled. "Now it's time for your bath." He used the homemade pulley system to maneuver the girl's body over an old porcelain tub. Slowly he lowered her body into the tub and began to rub salt into her skin. He covered her in the salt that filled the tub, humming an almost obscenely happy tune.

"Soon you'll be cured, and then you can join

your friends," he told her, but his words fell on dead ears.

That was the problem with women these days, they never really listened. Especially after they were dead.

Once he had the girl settled into the salt bath he turned his attention onto his other guests. He dragged the bodies out of the little room and over to a sheet-covered pillar. He let go of the last body with a rapturous rush of held breath and stared up at his latest creation. It was his crowning achievement, and he'd be damned if the art world was going to criticize this piece of work. He had become a regular Pygmalion, so in love with his work was he. With a flourish, he pulled the sheet from the pillar and let it float to the floor. He arranged the bodies upon the altar he had created, but to get them to look perfect, he would have to wait on his last guest to take her place in the procession.

Each day he rearranged his guests while he waited, placing each in the perfect angle so the light would hit them just right. Each day he added to his creation, until finally his last guest was ready.

"The Last Supper," he whispered, devotion spilling into his every action with the reverence of a worshipper new to the religion.

He lovingly set his last guest into place, twisting her head to an odd angle, the cracking bones spreading his fanatic's smile even wider across his pale drawn face. Two months of intense devotion to the new God had made him into a changed man. Two months without truly sleeping. He only hoped his sacrifice was acceptable so that God would let him rest. He wanted so much to rest. Becky hadn't understood what was going on. She blamed him for her inability to sleep, she didn't understand that God was punishing them for their sins. So she'd left him. She hadn't appreciated his sculpture that he now called "The Last Supper". She had screamed for such a long time that he had thought her head would have exploded. Much to his disappointment, it hadn't exploded, it just kept screaming.

"Shut up," he said flatly, the sound of his voice in the silence scaring the holy hell out of him.

It took him a second to realize he had been speaking to a memory. The guests were all in place now, and he began to paint them as they were, spreading the shellac in liberal strokes. He needed a chair to reach the top portions, and by then he was onto his third can. The scent of the coating was overpowering and he started to feel light-headed. Sniffing glue had done the same thing for him, but to a lesser degree. Probably the lack of sleep making the effect of the shellac fumes stronger. He had to work fast, though. He could feel the fume headache coming on in the back of his skull and right up where he pictured his nose probably connected to his brain.

After he'd piled on the first coat he decided to break for lunch and let the shellac dry. Wait until the bastard and bitch art critics in SoHo saw his latest creation. But then again, he supposed they were getting a first person point of view of it. It was better than that piece of shit that they'd called "art" that featured a crucifix in a jar of piss. Hell, it was better than a lot of what had been passing for art lately. Especially since the war had started. Who'd known there really were such things as vampires? Since the rioting had started two months ago he and Becky hadn't been able to sleep a wink. It was obvious that the undead bastard who had started the ball rolling really was a messenger from God, and that the human race was most certainly on its way to hell.

He took a step back to admire his work. It was beautiful, truly art. It made the ceiling of the Sistine Chapel look like a child's finger painting.

The faces were taut with fear and pain, limbs straining and intertwined to create a type of seat. At a glance it appeared the bodies were still moving. He had done such a wonderful job paying attention to detail. Each upturned face was an expression of contemporary life, and each body worked to create a throne fit for God.

They'd never say he lacked imagination again. They wouldn't be able to. He'd sealed their mouths shut. By the end of the second coat of shellac he wouldn't even be able to hear them screaming anymore.

A LETTER TO LIZ

By

Ann Ominous

Dear Nik,   November 3, 19—

Gonna have to keep this one short. Loved

your last letter, it cheered me up so much. It was just what I needed. Ate at this really nice restaurant the other night. If you ever come to the area, I highly recommend it.

Went to a Poe reading, too. It was great, and the place they held it in was amazing! And get this, I'd had a dream about the place for over a year before I'd ever even heard about it! Weird, huh? Other than that, my life has been pretty mundane lately—unless you'd like to hear about my cats? Didn't think so.

Oh, yeah, one more thing. I'm sending that picture you wanted of me. Sorry it isn't a very good one, but hope you enjoy.

Later!

LIZ

He closed his eyes and brought the letter close to his face, sniffing the light perfume of the incense she burned at home. It was a dark, spicy aroma, mingled with the faintest trace of her perfume that must have rubbed off her wrist while she wrote. It was more perfumey, more feminine than the scent of the incense. His heart picked up its pace in anticipation as he reached back into the envelope for the snapshot still enfolded in the paper. He'd left it in there without looking at it, denying himself until he'd finished reading her letter, savoring the wonderful agony of excitement.

She was incredible. Her auburn hair just barely brushed her shoulders and the sweater she wore in the picture dipped just low enough to show her collarbones and completely expose her long, slender neck. He only knew her eyes were gray because she had told him that. The snapshot of her was taken at night with a flash—too close a flash, she was more than slightly washed out—and her eyes were little more than reflections of red and black. Amateur photography, probably taken with a disposable point-and-click camera. It did not matter, her personality was captured perfectly in the photo, her smile wide and bright and REAL. It reached her eyes. One hand was posed behind her head, the sleeve of the sweater slipped down enough to expose one pale, washed-out wrist, but he could still see a scar running down her wrist like an inverted cross.

He felt the tears rising in the back of his throat and he choked them down again. So beautiful. He hung the picture over his desk and carefully folded the letter, placing it into a carved wooden box, on top of past letters he'd received from Elizabeth Channing, the love of his, Nikolas Miles, life. Someday he would tell her. Maybe soon. He grabbed a pen and paper and began to write.

Dearest Liz,   November 6, 19—

It was good to finally see you. You're very lovely. I mean that. Your boyfriend is a very lucky man.

I'm afraid I don't have much to say. My existence has been very mundane as of late, but I will make it up to you! I don't have any pictures to send, but I AM sending you the first draft of a story I'm writing. Tell me what you think, alright? And be honest, I can take it.

Until next time,

NIK

Liz smiled and felt herself still blushing at the compliment as she refolded the note and took out the manuscript he had sent her. An hour later she was putting another letter into the mailbox.

Dear Nik,   November 9, 19—

You're a sly one, I have to say. I don't have a boyfriend. There, I've said it. Satisfied? Now you know.

O.K. Next subject: your manuscript. Great! You should send it in to a publisher! I was really impressed. Your characters seemed to live and breathe and talk. My only problem is: Where the hell's the rest?!! You've left me hanging! Grr. At any rate, you've got my reaction.

So how are things with you in good ole Arizona? Dry, I'd imagine. The Poconos are getting pelted with huge rainstorms. It's really weird.

Last week we had snow! At least my roof is holding up. I should have probably put on a new roof this summer, but money was tight. Not that it still isn't, mind you, but now I've got a roof fund. Oh well.

I have to get to work soon, so I'll let you go for now.

> Later, 'gator.

> --- LIZ

P.S. If you don't feel like writing and want to call, or your hand gets mangled by a wild dog, gimme a call. I'm up at all hours, better that you call at night, but not between 7pm-8pm. And here's a big ole chap stick kiss to seal the letter, in return for your compliments.

He frowned slightly. What the hell did she do between seven and eight at night that she wouldn't take calls? It was going to bother him. And this letter smelled different. There was a definite aroma of... cinnamon? He stared at the lip-shaped smudge on the paper and smelled it. Cinnamon. A slow fire spread between his legs and he kissed the place that Liz had kissed. He licked his lips and got hard. He could taste the cinnamon now, on his lips and smell it. So sweet and good to eat. Just like Liz. She obviously wanted him, and if she didn't... well, there was no boyfriend hanging around....

He picked up the phone and began to make arrangements. Nik Miles was going to find his friend in Pennsylvania.

Liz opened her mailbox and smiled as she recognized the distinct scrawl of Nik's handwriting. He was a nice enough guy, although she had only his description of himself to go on as far as looks. Six feet tall, dark brown hair and brown eyes. She had responded to an ad he had placed in the back of a magazine for a pen pal, mainly just so she would have a friend who was not in Pennsylvania, to hear about the rest of the country. To know there was something *real* out there.

She piled the rest of the mail into her arms and turned Nik's envelope over in her hands. There was no postmark.

"That's odd," she said aloud into the crisp afternoon air.

Her voice sounded small and alone. With a shiver she hurried back up the road to her house.

Dearest Liz,   November 10, 19—

I've been extremely busy lately. I finished the story, and naturally I've sent you the rest of it. I wouldn't want you to keep twisting in the wind like some common corpse. I hope you enjoy the ending. I think you will.

I enjoyed the kiss. Does this mean you would consider me for the job of Boyfriend if I were to ask? I promise I'd be good and only go on the newspapers. Just something for you to consider. I am housebroken!

But, alas, I must cut this short. I have so much to do and of course no time to do it! Maybe I will give you a call one of these nights. By the way, what is you number? You forgot to include it in your last letter.

           Sincerely,

           NIK

P.S. What is it you do between 7pm and 8pm? Just curious.

     She shook her head and smiled slightly. He

could always make her laugh. But there was

something that bothered her, she just could not quite figure out what it was. The missing postmark was no big deal, that happened sometimes, but there was something else…. Better not to drive herself crazy. She would think of it later.

He watched her close the mailbox, barely able to keep from running over and checking to see if she had written him back. But he would wait. Soon he would let her know he was in town, and then he would tell her how he felt about her. When she was safely up the road and he had heard her porch door close he ran out of his hiding place in the ditch across the main road and practically tore open the mailbox. There it was, addressed to him, his letter. He ripped it open as he climbed into his rented car and sat behind the wheel, barely breathing.

Dear Nik,   November 11, 19—

I tore through the rest of the manuscript last night and I loved it! The way you ended it with a bang— literally, was sheer genius, and by the end I was in tears. Congrats on evoking emotions from me.

About the kiss… I just kind of put it there to be different, so my letter wouldn't be ordinary and blah. But I'm glad you enjoyed it. I'm not really looking for a boyfriend, however. My last one is still bothering me, so it's like we never really broke up, except now we ONLY fight. Nothing else. So… I've got my hands full with HIM, bastard that he is. He wasn't housebroken, but he DID break my house.

I'm still open for phone calls, though. Sorry I didn't give my numero in the last one. Guess I forgot. It's (717)555-2222. Too simple, right? I know, I've got the idiot's phone number, believe me. Drunk folks always call up with the wrong number.

As to what I do between 7 and 8pm—that's my secret. Heh heh heh…. 'Til later,   ----LIZ

He held the paper to his nose and sighed. This was so much better, the scent was stronger, more fresh. He started the car and drove past her house. She was out on the porch with a black and white cat. Cute. Would make a great picture. He pulled off the road just far enough past her house that he would be unnoticed and took out a camera with a telephoto lens.

He turned the focus ring until her face was framed in an incredible close-up shot. He snapped off a few frames of her, then zoomed out to a wider angle that included her cat. When he had finished the roll of film he shifted the car back to drive and pulled back around to pass her house again. Once more he stared out the window at her and she raised her hand in greeting. He returned the wave and drove on. He was tempted to leave a letter in her mailbox, but there were two reasons he would not. The first one: the mail had not yet been picked up, and the second: he had had no postmark on the last letter and the date he had just habitually written at the top of the letter was almost the same day she had sent it. If he kept that up she would catch on quickly. If she had not caught on already. He silently cursed himself for his own impatience. This letter he would just have to be patient. He would wait, and he would watch. There was a house across the street from her home that looked abandoned. If he had to, he could stay there for a little while. It might even be better that way. Then he could keep an even closer eye on her. Either way, he was definitely coming back that night to find out what it was she did between 7 and 8pm. But first he would write her a letter.

Dearest Liz,

I'm glad you enjoyed the story. I think I'll dedicate it to you, my first and only fan.

I'm sorry to hear about the troubles with the ex. If I was there, I'd protect you. A modern knight in shining armor. There we go. Chivalry has been resurrected!

I'm going to be doing some travelling in the near future, maybe even out your way if you'd like me to drop by. Don't worry, I'll call first so you can clean up, right?

And your phone number is not an idiot's phone number. I prefer to think of it as one that begs to be remembered and used frequently. A number that would give the caller's fingers immense pleasure just through dialing... ah... but to be on the receiving end of that open line and to view the lovely speaker... THAT would truly be ecstasy.

And with those parting words, I bid you adieu.

With all my hopes and dreams,

NIK

P.S. I've decided to start sending your letters in the overnight mail after this one so you will get them more quickly.

     He read and reread his letter, searching for any obvious or not-so-obvious discrepancies before finally nodding his silent approval. It was flawless. He could copy the postmark and then leave it in her mailbox about four days from now. He had to be very careful or he would be discovered. He checked the hotel room's clock and swore under his breath. Almost seven o'clock. He had to fly if he was going to make it to her house in time.

     And fly he did. At exactly seven he parked in the crumbling overgrown driveway of the house across the street. He sat with his hands tightly locked on the steering wheel, head bowed, waiting for his breathing to slow to normal. When it did, he got out of the car and waited practically on her front porch.

     At five after seven she came outside, triggered the motion light, and went down the stairs.

One of her cats, a small orange and white spotted model—a tom by the looks of him—came dashing out of the underbrush to join her.

"Simon!" she gasped, her look of momentary fear melting to happy surprise as she bent down to pet the mangy tomcat's head.

The strange pair made their way to the top of her driveway, the wet leaves muffling every footstep, still soggy from the rainstorms. That was in his favor. He could move through the woods without drawing too much notice to himself. Had they been dry leaves he would have been heard for miles in the still November night. That being the case, he might move into the abandoned house that night.

As she walked up the driveway the cat ran ahead of her and stopped, staring straight at him. He felt his stomach lurch in angry panic when Liz stopped behind her cat, attempting to see into the darkness.

"Simon, it's OK, baby-guy. See? Nothing there."

But her voice cracked with fear. She bent down and nudged the little tom gently, but he refused to move. Instead he continued to stare into the hiding place, and now he was growling deep in the back of his little feline throat.

Nik had never heard a cat growl, and it sent shivers up his spine followed by goosebumps. Then the cat started to meow at him, angry in an unexplainably eerie way, as if questioning and outraged by his very existence. Damned if he almost answered that challenging question. And then an idea came to him. He meowed back, just as angrily, and Liz visibly relaxed.

"It's just another cat, you crazy thing. Nearly gave me a heart attack! C'mon. We'll go this way then."

She picked up Simon, much to his dislike, and carried him to the other side of the driveway. When she put him down he turned to stare back at the enemy.

"Simon, that's enough. Let's go."

Simon reluctantly followed, but kept turning back to stare at him with open hate. He would have to take care of that little beast. He was no idiot, he hsd seen all the Stephen King movies and others like them where the cats and various other pets always "protect" their owners by somehow maiming the "intruder". If the cat refused to be friends when he finally came to visit, he would just have to kill it.

First things first, he had to follow Liz and find out what she was doing. He could make out the grayish glow of the cat in what little light there was from the crescent moon that occasionally managed to blow through the racing clouds and he crept along as quietly as possible, matching his footfalls to hers.

She walked to the crossroads by her house and turned left onto the eastern branch. This road was more dirt and gravel than pavement. It was going to be hard for him to walk quietly. He stayed toward the edge of the road where there was a fair amount of moss and grass, it would help him to keep quiet and give him a better chance at hiding in the underbrush if she happened to look back.

Several times her little tom stopped and glared back at him, and she urged him forward until they reached a circular clearing. It was here that the road dead-ended into a cul-de-sac. The entire circle was covered over by polished gravel that glowed an unsettling gray in the night light. Liz walked to the center of the circle and stopped. Almost instantly a faint wind sprang up. She seemed to glow as her head fell back and the wind blew stronger. Soon dead leaves whipped around her in circular gusts that chilled him to the bone. He stared in awe as her glow became stronger and the wind reached a screaming crescendo. An aura of some dark type of anti-light surrounded her and she fell to her knees after a few moments of encasement by the blackness, the sound of the gravel crunching beneath her ringing out like a gunshot in the sudden silence. A small whimper escaped her as she fell forward onto her hands.

He did not notice immediately that his mouth was open, and when he did he shut it slowly, wondering how long it had been hanging open like a door to a haunted house. Whatever had been happening to her, it was over now. Simon broke her trancelike state with a small meow that seemed to suggest they get back. If that cat could have talked, it probably would have told its mistress about the stranger that was following her. Good thing the cat had gotten its own tongue....

He hid as she and Simon started back for her house. She passed so close to him that he could smell her perfume very faintly in the cold night air. It was musky, but not store-bought. She wore oils. The scent was captivating, dark and mysterious, just like her.

So many questions went through his mind, and now that he knew vaguely what she did during her hour of power, so-to-speak, he could ask her the others soon. Very soon.

He watched the sun rise the next morning. He had not slept at all that night. Had not slept for a long time. If he got an hour in for one night he considered himself lucky. He stared, zombielike, after the mailman's truck and then looked to the envelope he was holding. His postmark was perfect. Everything was set.

He opened her mailbox and put his letter on top of the pile of mail, then stopped. The corner of an envelope toward the center of the stack caught his eye. He pulled out her mail and began to glance through it. Mostly bills and catalogs, but there were two letters that he quickly shoved into his coat after perusing their main bodies. They were from *men*. He felt acid from his stomach rising up to burn the back of his throat. The first letter was from her ex. He had threatened her in it, and now that Nik had... Larry Johnson's name and address, he would make him pay dearly for trying to upset Liz.

The second letter was what finally caused his stomach to heave its acid rain into the roadside brush. The man in the letter was very... personal. He wanted to take Liz away. He would not be able to convince her to leave with him if she never got his letter, though. As for Larry Johnson... he was going to have a little chat with him.

Liz jumped slightly as the crashing ring of
the phone shattered the tomblike silence. She quickly
shut the novel she had been reading and grabbed the
phone, already full of dread at who might be calling.

"Hello?"

"It's me."

"Hi, Larry. What do you want now?"

"Don't be a bitch, you were always such a
bitch—."

"*What*... do you want."

"I want you to keep your pet psycho the hell
away from me."

"My WHAT? Look, I have no idea—."

"Yeah, alright. I'm only gonna say this once
you stupid twat. He tries to hurt me, I hurt *you*. Got
it?"

"But I—Hello?"

She closed her eyes and sighed when the dialtone followed the click. What the hell was he talking about? Unless... the thing from the cul-de-sac had managed to get loose? She shivered and pulled her sweater tighter to her throbbing throat. If that thing ever got loose, they were all in for it.

Nik smiled, almost laughed with glee, when Larry put down the phone and stared again in silent rage at the note. Larry just did not understand the sheer beauty of a well-written death threat. He clapped both his hands over his mouth and began shifting his weight from foot to foot in an impatient dance while Larry went to lock the front door. Paranoid bastard. If he only knew that he'd just locked himself in with what he had tried to lock out. Gave new meaning to deadbolts.

The next evening Liz only sighed when the phone rang.

"Hello?"

"Is this Liz?"

"Yes... who is this?"

"Nik."

"Nik? …Oh, NIK! Hi! Didn't think I'd ever hear from you! …Does this mean your hands got mangled?"

He laughed and blew out the candle by his telescope. "No, no… I just wanted to say hello and see if it would be alright to drop by soon."

"Drop by? You're coming out to Pennsylvania?"

"Yep."

"Well, yeah, I guess it would be alright."

He could see her pacing behind the sheer curtains draping the sliding glass door and he smiled through the trees and across the road from her home, from the abandoned house.

"Good. I'll see you soon."

He turned the cellular off quickly and waited. She would have another call coming in shortly about Larry.

When the phone rang again almost the

second after she had hung it up, Liz was more than curious.

"Nik? You forgot to ask for—."

"Miss Channing?"

"Yes...."

"This is John Trask with the Sheriff's Department. I have some bad news. About Lawrence Johnson. He committed suicide late last night."

"H—how?"

"He hanged himself. In the bathroom."

"Dear God...."

"Ma'am?"

She blinked. "N—nothing... I ... don't feel very well."

She hung the phone up almost unconsciously. It was a lie. Larry had been too selfish and too self-centered to have killed himself. He had been murdered by something else. She was going to settle it once and for all.

She pulled on her coat as she rushed out the door. The air was cold and the night was unusually dark as she stepped onto the deck and turned to close the porch door.

"Nice night for a walk, isn't it?"

She jumped, slamming the door home, its crash like the breaking of old bones in the night. She strained to see into the blackness by the stairs at the end of the deck and could just barely make out the dull glow of Simon's fur. The sound of footsteps moving slowly closer accompanied the triggering of the light, but only her half of the deck was thrown into the white-light. The other side of the deck where the footsteps were originating from was still in deep shadow after a momentary flash of white. The light had blown, leaving behind an eerie afterimage of a man in a long, dark trenchcoat.

"Who's there?" Liz squeaked, fumbling blindly for a weapon—any weapon.

"It's me, Liz…. It's Nik."

She relaxed only slightly as Nik stepped into

the light. What the hell was he doing there?

Simon growled at him and arched his back. Nik barely gave the little tom a passing glance when he kicked it. Damned cats. He *hated* cats.

"Simon!" Liz shrieked.

She stared in horror at her fallen would-be hero. The cat only stared at her, taking in small shallow breaths of air as it lay on its side.

"Why did you do that, you bastard?"

He inwardly flinched when she turned wide, accusing eyes onto him, then he hardened again.

"I've seen all the movies, I know what pets are capable of."

"You're *sick*...," she breathed, backing away from him. "You need help, Nik. You really do."

"I killed Larry for you, and *this* is the thanks I get?"

She stopped, her mouth falling open. "*You* did it?"

He nodded proudly.

He had forgotten all about the second cat, and she was much more experienced with stalking her prey than Simon. She waited for him on the deck railing, her black fur blending into the night while her bright yellow eyes watched and hated.

When Liz climbed up and over the railing to jump, Mittens attacked. She jumped straight for his eyes, the extra toes on her paws tearing at any place that would do damage. He screamed in pain and threw the cat off of him. She flipped and landed on her feet and disappeared into the night. He cursed and rubbed at the gashes left behind on his face then ran to the railing. Liz was already at the top of the driveway and running into the night. It did not matter. He knew where she was going, and now her pets were out of the way.

He followed her to the cul-de-sac, pausing only slightly when he saw the beginnings of the glow over the rise. The witch would be unable to perform spells without her familiars though, now would she not? No.

When he reached the top of the rise and saw what awaited him, he screamed. The glow had grown to the strength of stadium lights and he could just barely make out Liz's silhouette in the center.

The howls of the damned seemed to emanate from the light as it circled in waves around Liz and he grimaced at the pain of the light and sound. It felt as if it was all around him—IN him, through him. Then he realized that it *was* all around him. He had kept walking forward, completely unaware of what he was doing until he stood in the screaming light, in front of Liz.

Suddenly he knew the source of the light. It wasn't from Liz. It was from the thing that fed off her neck. Her eyes were wide, dead, and staring straight into his, telling him of the fate awaiting him in the unnatural angle of her head.

"Shit," he breathed.

More aspects were coming into focus as his pupils shrunk to the size of pinpricks. Liz's body floated over a foot off the ground, her neck level with the mouth of her murderer. The thing looked up from the wound and straight at him. Nik felt himself screaming from far away when the vampire—it could only be called by that name—seemed to smile and dropped Liz's body. Then it came toward him.

"You are my freedom, mortal. Accept your fate."

The words were cheesy as hell, but when they came from that bloody, reconnected throat they became horrifyingly real. He tried to run, but he was already dead.

November 20, 19—

Thanatos is free. And so am I, now. If all he's told me is true, God help us all.

Liz stared at the words on the page without blinking. Her mind still felt numb from death, but it was clearing. She heard a small scratching at the door and looked up to see her two cats waiting for her accompanied by the formerly imprisoned vampire named Thanatos. They had finished burying Nik in the garden behind Thanatos's old house, the one across the street. Now there would be two abandoned houses on the road. It was time to go.

She closed her diary and grabbed her bags. If anyone cared to break in, they would find the whole story of what had happened to her and her neighbor held within those pages. The story had only just begun for her, though. Now it was time to find out what Forever held.

THE MAN TO FEAR: AN

INTERVIEW WITH NEMESIS

by

Suzi M.

The lights glared down from the iron gridwork, turning the ceiling into a squared spiderweb of plumbing and Nemesis squinted in the white light of gelled heat. Too hot and too bright. He was used to perpetual winter and darkness. Suddenly he felt annoyed. Extremely annoyed.

"So tell us, Mr.……."

He turned his attention to the blonde reporter. "Nemesis."

"Mr. Nemesis—"

"No, just Nemesis." He smiled at the interviewer and she shifted uncomfortably under his emerald stare.

"Ah, yes… well then, *Nemesis*," she said it like she didn't believe it was his real name, like he was hiding behind an alias, "you are the man who started the war?"

He nodded.

"And would you mind telling us exactly *why* you started a war that cost thousands—even *millions* of innocent lives?"

"I was bored."

Stunned silence. Whatever clever cross-examination the reporter had had up her sleeve was now jammed in her throat, blocking words and air. She hadn't expected him to just agree to his actions, she expected a fight, a belligerent denial. Finally an outraged gasp and cough cleared her vocal chords and she changed her mask from self-righteous media-whore to judge-jury-and executioner-for-the United States of America.

"How *could* you?" she seethed. Her expertly painted features twisted and ran through a professional sampler of anger, shock, and fear. "There were *children* killed."

Nemesis nodded, remembering one very annoying little girl who had made her first mistake in getting too close to him and subsequently going on to getting too close to the edge of one of the two tallest buildings in New York City. "Yes," he finally said. "I know. I did them a favor. They won't have to live to see just how many real monsters there are in the world."

More shocked silence. Apparently Miss Rachel Gibson had expected a repent-and-forgive speech, one with lots of tears and stories of crimes of passion and a troubled childhood. She had expected him to turn that loaded, accusing, pointing finger at himself and to plead her acceptance and pity. Instead he'd pointed that smoking finger at his own victims, and then at the rest of the nation like some fucked up Darwinist. If she had been quick enough, she could have crucified him on National Television, but timing was everything, and she'd stumbled one too many times on her path of sorrows. Now she was pinned under her media cross.

Nemesis was getting bored, and he ruminated on a few simple facts. First fact: Rachel Gibson was not a natural blonde. Second fact: Nemesis hated blondes. Third fact: he hated people who weren't originally blonde who bleached their hair to become blonde even more than he hated the real thing. Something about that hair color was like waving a huge red blanket in front of a bull. Except that in bullfights the bull was contained in an arena, and Nemesis was free to wander the streets and china shops, even more free to impale would-be bullfighters. He turned bright, emerald green, hating eyes on the reporter, and a small twitching smile pushed at the corners of his mouth. Someone at the network must have really liked him to offer him a sacrifice.

Rachel noticed the hint if a smile and every nerve clanged out a regular four alarm. This guy was more than "a little weird in the head" as her superiors had suggested, he was fucking psychotic. The silence grew and she glanced at the black hulking forms of the cameras just barely visible beyond the three-point light-cage. Her producer waved his hands anxiously, pushing her to continue. And then she knew the question to nail her crazy friend to the wall.

"Don't you care about *anyone*? Isn't there anyone you *love* that could have been hurt by this insanity you've started? Or is it all just *you*? You don't give a damn about anyone but yourself, do you?"

"That's not true at all, Rachel," Nemesis answered quietly, and this time it wasn't only Rachel who was terrified by him, the crew and the entire live studio audience collectively wished they were anywhere but on that set. Rachel shifted uncomfortably, wondering if her sweat marks were visible to the cameras yet.

"I have someone I love VERY…MUCH." It was almost a challenge.

And that's when Rachel Gibson decided to get on a ratings high. Security could save her from the lion she was caged with. Nemesis, or whatever this guy's *real* name was, was getting upset. She'd managed to finally find the weak spot in his previously flawless armor, and she'd poked him. Now she was going in for the kill.

"Another victim of yours? Decided to take time off from the beatings and murder to try a little rape?" She glanced at her producer, who was now giving a thumbs-up sign, and then back to her "guest". His eyes seemed to be glowing green now, and the shadows that had surrounded his large eyes had become almost black. She glanced down at his black-gloved hands and her eyes widened. He'd clenched his hands to the point that the arms of the chair had crumbled beneath his grasp. She could only imagine how he must have wished the arms had been her neck.

"*Whore…*," he whispered. His deep voice dropped even lower, a large cat limbering for the pounce.

"*Excuse me?*" she tried to sound angry and indignant, but deep inside she felt almost ashamed, and more than a little afraid of him and what he might know.

"You heard me, you filthy bitch," Nemesis growled. "What right do *you* have to accuse *me*? You and your audience are so curious to know about *my* private life, but I think your horizontal climb up the professional ladder would be much more to their tastes, don't you?" The smile that had twitched only slightly before was now the huge shark-smile of a madman.

Rachel Gibson, all-American girl-next-door, whose image was her main career, growled, "How do you know that? Who told you?"

And her audience gasped as if on cue.

"No one told me. I didn't *need* anyone to tell me. And to answer your question from before, yes, I *do* love someone. That someone is my wife. She is the first and only woman I've ever loved and ever *will* love. I was about to end the fighting, at *her* request.

She begged me to end it, and I would have. I love her enough to put her happiness before mine. And then a lynch mob found her trying to save a child's life...."

Despite her fear and hatred of the man Rachel listened in wide-eyed wonder. A *wife*? Who the hell would actually *marry* this guy? Yes, he was incredibly gorgeous, and those *eyes*, Jesus! When Rachel had first met him she'd had an almost overwhelming urge to fuck him on the spot, but she'd reminded herself of who and what he was. He was right up there with Hitler socially, and yet there was just something so sexy and innocent about him. And when he talked about his wife the expression on his face told that he more than just loved her. He *worshipped* her. Rachel was surprised to hear herself ask gently, "What happened to her?"

Nemesis looked at her for a moment and she felt all of his pain and anger. All of his hate for mortals.

"They beat her almost to death, then staked her and hung what they'd thought was her dead body from a lamp post."

"Oh, oh Jesus," Rachel whispered, one hand travelling a shaking path to her mouth. The audience and crew held a collective breath as Nemesis glared at them all, daring them to feel pity for him.

"She was still ALIVE...," he groaned, "Somehow she managed to get down, perhaps someone was disgusted enough to cut her down. She isn't even sure. When she came home, her knees were bloody from crawling. She *crawled home* because she was in too much pain to stand and walk!

"Nivek, my servant, carried her to our bedroom. He had found her on the steps of our home, unconscious and weak from bloodloss. They tried to hide her from me so that I wouldn't see what your kind had done to her, but nothing could keep me away from her. When I finally saw her… she had partially healed, but I could still *feel* her pain and fear… I swore revenge, for her, it's what I do, and the war continued."

Nemesis an old and tired god, looked at his captive audience and laughed bitterly as he ran a hand through his unkempt black hair. "*I* didn't even start the physical violence! I only planted the seed of a revolution. It took a group of panicked mortals to actually start the fighting." His smile felt like it was splitting his face in half. "It was the vampires at that gathering who tried to control the violence and save the lives of mortals!"

He couldn't stop laughing for a moment. Just

the thought of the war the mortals had started and pinned on *him*. It was too funny. He had just wanted a revolution, the

violence and bloodshed had been merely a pleasant side-effect. He finally got his laughter under control and sneered at his audience. "But *I'm* the monster...."

Rachel lowered her eyes, feeling suddenly ashamed and guilty. She had seen the unedited footage of the Incident in Washington Square, and Nemesis was right, the mortals *had* started it. The networks had conveniently overlooked or outright lied about that little fact. They had taken Nemesis on the show to introduce an all-around scapegoat, inciter, mass-murderer, and war criminal, and now the half of America that was still alive and staying tuned in was probably hanging their heads in shame.

He stared out into the faces of millions of television viewers and shook his head. "When I was a god, things were much better. Now, if you will all excuse me, I would like to go home."

"Wait!"

Nemesis turned back to face the reporter, a small frown of annoyance beginning. The shadows played over his face and he straightened up from his slouch to his full height of six feet, nine inches. The crowd took a surprised breath and he knew what they were thinking: he was much bigger in person. He arched an eyebrow expectantly and said, "Yes?"

"You never finished.... What happened to your wife?"

Nemesis sighed and his body fell into a slouch again as if a heavy weight had been lifted and then replaced. He glared at the reporter and then at the audience. "She died for your sins, and when she came back to me the woman I loved was gone. I'm still waiting for her to come back to me.... Losing her was my punishment, moreso than my imprisonment. What good is freedom when everything that made you alive is gone?" He choked on his own sarcasm and pain and felt the hate rising in him again, but he was too tired to act on it. At one time he would have killed the entire crew and audience on live television and still had enough kick to entertain the viewers at home, now all he had left was frustration and sadness. He sneered at the cameras and at Rachel Gibson. "I hope this was what you were expecting, Miss Gibson. Once again, goodbye. And Miss Gibson?"

"Yes?"

"A word of advice for you and anyone else who cares to listen. Try to keep in mind that if there's no one there with you that you care for when you finally get to the "top" as you say, success makes for a very cold bedfellow. Caring for someone is the greatest experience I've ever known. I haven't lost it, I lost the essence of my devotion. Remember that nothing is stable, and the more power you attain, the less stable your life will become. My advice to you is to think about what you really want. Power and perfection are not the same thing, and you will never get them both since power automatically corrupts perfection."

THE UPSTAIRS ROOM

By

James Glass

She sat perfectly still, listening to the wind
blow through her body, completely numb from the
cold December dusk and starving. She watched the

people below passing by with mildly interested boredom. In her mind, only one word flashed: tonight. As soon as the sun sank below the horizon, he would arrive… he would feed her. She let her head fall against the thick soundproof glass of the window, tinted so that she could see out and no one could see in.

She turned to face into the room and watched her shadow grow, longer and longer, then finally fade. The room was dark now. She let her breath out slowly and closed her eyes (so tired) as the doorknob turned. He was here… her salvation.

"Hello, pretty thing."

She stared blankly at the looming shadow speaking to her from the darkness. What was he saying? She didn't care. All that mattered was that he was pulling off his shirt. Exposing his neck.

"Are you hungry?"

His voice was low and hypnotic and his eyes glinted like steel. The cold calculating cruelty was a welcome change to no company at all. She sighed and rested her head on her shoulder. Yes, she was hungry. Hungry for nourishment and starving for someone to keep her company. She wanted to be among the living again.

"Vampires are all alike," he told her, his glittering silver gaze resting on her. "They want to live forever and die for eternity…. But *you*," he laughed at her, "You are different, are you not, beautiful one?"

His white dress shirt was off now and she couldn't help staring at the way his black slacks hugged his hips, moving with his stride. He was so beautiful. His silver eyes followed her wanton stare and his jaw clenched in anger.

"Do you want me now, undying mortal? Do you want me in the way I have wanted you?" He held his shimmering white arms out in offering, and a strand of his raven-black hair fell across his hollowly handsome face. "Am I so beautiful to you now?"

His angelic mouth twisted into a wry smile

as he leaned over her as if to kiss her. She stared at his eyes, his dark-light, his exposed neck, and she licked her lips. The hunger rose in her, becoming too strong…. He smiled.

"Drink."

It was all the invitation she needed. His silver eyes opened wide in the darkness as her teeth pierced him, agony and ecstasy welling and ebbing on a chaotic tide within him. Then the familiar drunken feeling and she held him in her arms, caressing him as his silvery white blood dripped from her chin, her face as cherubic as the day he had found her… he found himself laughing at the thought of himself in the arms of his own angel of death.

"Sweet Azrael… I love you," she whispered to him, kissing him lightly on the cheek as she stroked his hair away from his face.

"I know," he answered, his silver eyes staring into her golden eyes, "Your kind always do." He stroked her long black hair and traced her lips with a long slender finger. "I must go."

He felt her arms tighten around him and a darkness flickered behind her eyes. She nodded slowly and her pretty lips twisted in contempt.

"I know," she spat, "You always leave me here, all alone… *starving*." She pushed him out of her arms. "I hate you," she rasped.

Azrael put his shirt on and began to fasten it. She could see his jaw muscles working in anger and she sighed.

"You would be well-advised to refrain from arousing my wrath," he hissed, tugging at the buttons of his shirt, emphasizing each word with the button.

She stared at him and he turned away from her. She watched his back instead, looking at his broad shoulders and thin waist. His silvery white skin appeared jaundiced in the sodium glow of the streetlamps outside the window. She stood and placed her hands on her hips, the first slow kindlings of anger rising up in her throat.

"*You* would be well-advised to let me go, Azrael."

"I'll be back soon," he told her quietly, kissing her smooth, cool forehead. No words of sarcasm or anger from her this time. She merely dropped her eyes and nodded.

"What is your name?"

She looked back up at him in surprise. He had never asked her, and she had just assumed that he knew what her name was. His hands caressed her face and he smiled.

"You are not dead yet. I know only those that are in my realm.... Will you tell me?"

"Lucretia."

"Beautiful. Goodbye, Lucretia."

She watched him leave with a growing sense of uneasiness and sadness. It had been one week since he had taken her to this prison and it felt like it was going to be an eternity. Lucretia slid down the wall and rested her head on her knees. Who was she kidding? It *was* going to be an eternity. An eternity with the Angel of Death. How ironic.

The next evening she woke to find Azrael already there, watching her. The sunset made the room a strange golden-gray through the tinted glass of the window and Lucretia squinted into the dimness. She could just make out the silver glow of his eyes.

"Good evening, Lucretia."

"Hello."

She pushed herself up on one elbow and regarded him levelly. He stood up from his crouch and moved into the growing glow of the streetlamps. Little by little his body came into view, until the light finally fell onto his face. His eyes glittered coldly under his thin black eyebrows. He went to his knees next to her and smiled.

"How old are you?"

Lucretia paused then finally said, "One hundred and twenty years old."

She'd had to think about that one. It had been so long since she'd had to figure out her own age. Azrael smiled again.

"How did you come to be a vampire?"

It was her turn to smile now. The memory of that night tearing across her mind, the way the shadows fought over her....

"It was 1899, I was twenty... he later became my husband."

"I see. So where is he now?"

"He was killed in the war." Lucretia sighed.

The war. She had almost forgotten the war now, too. She could have been killed.

"Which war?" Azrael asked as he took a seat on the floor next to her.

She stared at him incredulously. "What do you *mean* 'which war'?!" She tried not to sound agitated, but it was no use.

"Just as I've said. You forget how many battles I have seen in my time." Azrael smiled at her, but there was no humor in it.

She sighed and nodded, absently brushing a stray strand of hair away from her face. "The Immortal War. There was a vampire scare and the mortals went insane. It was like the Inquisition and the Salem Witch Trials rolled into one…. They murdered so many innocents."

"Ah, yes, I know the one."

Lucretia glanced up at him as she twisted the silk sheets from her makeshift bed. Her hands felt numb and detached as a spark of anger flared deep inside of her. She frowned at Azrael's angelic smiling face.

"How can you be so unemotional about that? Don't you care that people are suffering and dying as we speak?!"

Lucretia was standing now, her hands curled into fists, eyes blazing like hellfire. The emotional numbness was gone. Already she could feel her face tingling with fury. Azrael's smile returned and suddenly he was also standing.

"You forget who and what I am. I am the

Angel of Death. Nothing more, nothing less. If I began to feel for those I must take, then only a very few would die," he held his hands out in a half-shrug, "so you see, it is my responsibility not to have feelings… normally I make it my mission to see that it stays that way." Azrael's smile faded as he became serious. "You are the exception to my rules. Normally I enjoy taking your kind, so pompous and arrogant, believing they'll live forever because they're immortal by mortal standards. Idiots. *No one escapes me.*"

"I am well aware of that fact," Lucretia growled in frustration, falling back onto the bed.

She returned his angry stare and felt her anger already turning to the familiar fear. She hated this whole situation.

"Why do you insist on angering me, Lucretia? Do you not realize that I can make eternity a very miserable thing?"

He was almost pleading with her now, his hands held out, palms up. Lucretia snorted and stared up at the ceiling.

"Go away. You're not a god... don't try to pretend that you are.... You're just like the rest of us, forgotten and misunderstood."

She turned her head to glare up at him, but he made no move to leave, just stood there with his jaw working in silent anger.

"What are you staring at?? I said go away!"

She could hear the shrillness creeping into her voice. Too shrill. Too scared. So tired.

He turned on her and drove her against a wall. She felt a long-forgotten panic as his hands tightened on her. For an instant she was in another time, it was dark, with a darker figure pushing her to the floor, hands groping and hurting, voice growling in her ear "Stay still, bitch!" The shadow was attacked by another and killed before her eyes. The second shadow had gone on to become her husband. The first shadow had been the town sheriff. Every time she heard the sound of keys in a lock she automatically threw her hands up to protect her face and move to the nearest darkest corner.

The past melted away and she was caught in Azrael's curious gaze. He stared at her for a long time, then asked quietly, "Where were you?"

He didn't like the darkness in her eyes, the way she feared certain things. She feared his anger, and she was afraid he would hurt her

"I was here, getting harassed by you."

She frowned and struggled against his embrace. He held her tighter and kissed her. She spat on him and wiped her mouth.

"I'll be back soon," he told her quietly, kissing her cool forehead as if nothing had happened. This time no words of sarcasm or anger. She dropped her eyes in defeat.

Azrael looked at her. She was clutching the sheets to her as if he was about to rape her and he frowned. What had happened to her before he'd found her? What had she seen, and who had made her this way?

"You should have let me die."

She slowly slid up the wall, hidden by the shadows and still clutching the sheet to herself like a shroud. Azrael remained silent. He remembered the day he had found her.

"Burning yourself at the stake did not seem to be your style," he told her.

"I don't care! ... I was ready to die. You should have let me die," her voice fell to a rasping whisper and she bunched the sheets up as she spoke.

He watched her carefully; he knew about the insanity buried in the vampires. Their high levels of intelligence literally drove them mad, and Lucretia was currently the perfect case study.

"You must be hungry," he tried, but she only sank further into the shadows. When he reached out to touch her she clawed him, leaving long gashes down his arms.

A flash of blinding white light lit up where she hid and threw her against the wall. When she could see again Azrael was standing over her, frowning.

"*Never* do that again," he said simply, his voice low and threatening.

She smiled up at him through the flowers of white light that bloomed and exploded in front of her eyes. "What are you going to do about it? What? *Kill* me? Go ahead! That was the whole point to begin with, remember?"

He closed his eyes in exasperation, remembering all too well the way she had been standing on the roof of the building she had set on fire. She had had all the implements of a pyro around her, with her arms stretched out to embrace the flames. As he had watched, she had made her way toward an old television antenna. He had gotten to her just as she'd impaled herself, and she'd been smiling....

She had been too much of a curiosity to pass up. One of the undead *trying* to kill herself. And she was one of the most beautiful women he had ever seen... and he was tired of being alone.

"This has to stop."

Azrael turned back to Lucretia, confusion filling his silver eyes. She was sitting serenely in the corner, shrouded in shadows.

"What has to stop?" he asked innocently. She fell onto her side and lay still.

"You'll see."

Azrael didn't *want* to see. She refused to tell him any more, though. For the next week and a half he could only watch her.

Lucretia waited for him to leave again before setting her plan in motion. He had been constantly with her during the last week and a half, never letting her out of his sight for more than a moment. She had stopped drinking from him, and he scolded her repeatedly, but she was resolute. No more.

Now she scrounged around the small apartment, gathering odds and ends. Mostly ends. An old coat rack, broken in half, was a more wonderfully jagged point than she could have planned, along with a claw hammer, a Bible, a crucifix, garlic from the kitchen, a large glass jar, and some water to put in it. She had had to stop and rest during the gathering process numerous times, her strength running out of her as if she had been bleeding herself. Now she was set. She threw the Bible, the garlic, and the crucifix into the jar of water and set it carefully on the windowsill, flinching at the discomfort the sunlight caused her skin, then she sat down and waited for high noon.

Soon enough the noon sun shone in, hot and fiery, and a little too soon for her taste. It was now or never, though. If she didn't do it now, Azrael would be coming soon to check on her and she'd miss her chance. She moved to the window, holding the jagged coatrack-turned-stake in one hand and the hammer in the other. She set them down in the sun and lifted her jar of what she hoped would be holy water and spilled some onto her stake, dumping the remainder onto herself. She was surprised she didn't just burst into flames from touching the holy objects, much less pouring them all over her. Maybe it didn't work because there was no God waiting at the end of it all. It didn't matter, she'd find out soon enough. The stake was what really mattered.

She positioned the stake over her heart, then sent it home with a quick smack of the hammer. The intense pain was more than she had planned, and the rush of crimson from the wound in her chest was more than she expected, but death was rarely pleasant. She only had a few minutes before Azrael showed up now, and she had to work faster to annihilate her body in order to free her soul.

Lucretia faced the noon sunlight from across the room like a showdown in a western, and she ran headlong toward the thick tinted glass. Straight at the window and then through it, falling into the familiar ocean of Society, with its tide of curious faces all turned upward to see what all the commotion was about. Lucretia smiled and waved.

The impact was also drastically underestimated, she thought briefly in the seconds before her skull cracked open like an egg against the hot black asphalt of the street. Finally, sweet oblivion. Thank God, she would finally die. Lucretia closed her eyes, enjoying the warm burn of the sun on her face.

Azrael made his way through the crowd of curious onlookers, inconspicuous to all. No one ever noticed him. As he came up to his latest kill, he shook his head in disbelief and protest. On the street before him was a splattered version of his lovely Lucretia. As he stood over her she opened her blood-filled eyes and stared up at him, defiant in a dead sort of way. He shook his head at her, sadness filling him.

"No," he whispered as she smiled and closed her eyes. He still loved her.

"Too bad," a bystander was saying, and Azrael turned to stare at them with ice-cold lifeless eyes, "She was really pretty."

"How can you tell?" another asked with disgust, "It's a stain on the street!"

Azrael closed his eyes and tried to ignore

them, their mortal disregard for the dead sickening and angering him. He should take them all, there and then, show them what it was they made lightly of.

"Azrael."

He opened his eyes, silver flashing in the golden sunlight. Lucretia stood before him, next to her broken remains. Again he shook his head. "Lucretia, please. I cannot let you go."

"But you *have* to!" she cried, "You're *Death*. It's your job…. Please, Azrael, I want this. My time was up a long time ago."

He dropped his head in resignation. He hated his job, dammit, and now, without Lucretia to come home to, he would be alone. Again.

"Come to me." He held his long white arms out to her. No great billowing black cloak, no skull for a head, no scythe. He was just Azrael. The Angel of Death. Nothing more, nothing less.

For the first time since he had found her Lucretia walked willingly into his embrace and gently kissed him. He held her close and felt her drifting away, could already see her in the next world with her lost friends and relatives. It was a bright place, with happy shouts of recognition and laughter. For a moment he remembered Eden.

Lucretia turned to look back and raised a hand to him in farewell. Azrael held his own up in return.

"Goodbye."

He felt the light fade, felt the gloominess of the world settling back upon him as the doorway melted away. The world was so much darker to him now.

He walked into the late afternoon, slowly working his way toward sunset. He began to feel his age, millennium upon millennium hanging heavily upon his thin frame. For the first time in eons he held his scythe, but only for support as he parted the cold sea of hostile faces. This time they all saw him.

THE VIGILANTE PSYCHIC

By

XIRCON

Rain spattered the New York City streets and dripped acid into his upturned eyes. It stung like hell, but he was used to it. Every night was an insane repetition of the nights before it anyway. Back to watching, his black eyes piercing the night.

The man in the overcoat shivered as he walked past, a prime target for Erik. Erik the Vigilante Psychic. Ordinary Erik couldn't do this type of thing; waiting in the rain, watching New York rot from her inside out. The only thing Ordinary Erik watched was too much TV, eating his microwave dinners, gaining too much weight, happy in his mundane existence.

"Was she good?"

The man in the overcoat stared up at Erik, terror bleaching his face as white as his hair. "wh— Who?" he squeaked. Guilty.

"The woman. The one you raped and killed," Erik said as he leaned in closer to the man, his already deep voice dropping to menacing, "Was she good?"

"I –I don't know who you're talking about! I haven't killed or raped anyone!" The man began to back away slowly, finally breaking into a terrified run. Erik caught up to him easily, jumped, caught an overhanging tree branch, swung, and landed in front of the man.

"Stanley," he hissed, "Your name is Stanley Borden. Isn't it?"

The man went even paler, his eyes wide with fear. What the hell *was* this guy chasing him?

"ISN'T IT?" Erik repeated, "Speak up, don't make me beat it out of you. I'd really like to, you know." The man in the overcoat whose name was Stanley Borden nodded, staring in fear at Erik's black eyes, dark brown hair, and above average stature and build. A little on the chunky side, he would tell police when he got away.

"And didn't you rape and kill a young woman not too long ago?"

Stanley Borden nodded.

Erik reached behind him and pulled out his trusty weighted aluminum baseball bat. He could have used wood, but wood breaks and wood stains.

Aluminum is forever. "I have something for you."
Erik smiled.

Stanley tried to run, but his legs were smashed before he could even take a step. Faster than he could scream, duct tape was sealed over his mouth and wrapped around his head, closing off his cries for help and cutting off his air supply. Black-gloved hands finished wrapping the rest of Stanley's head—less blood dripping all over and less to clean up. Duct tape was virtually waterproof if done the right way. A heavy metallic thud and Stanley Borden was put to justice.

JOURNAL ENTRY #1

ToNight makes 5. Only 5. The first WAS a thief, stealing from the poor & the rich. I stopped him when he began stealing lives. The 2ND was a woman who killed her children watching them drown in the bathtub Crying for her THE IMAGES!! OH GOD MAKE THEM **STOP**!!! I'm better.------ the third – the most disturbing. A child. Killed his own parents & set the apartment on FIRE. They were tied to the bed because they'd taken his away—The 4th was a mugger in Central Park .He robbed and raped the joggers. BASTARD! He WON'T DO IT AGAIN.

Tonight's WASTE was DESPICABLE. He had RAPED & murdered a woman after slipping a drug into her drink. His only regret about killing her was that he might get caught. **MY** only regret is that I didn't catch him sooner.

JOURNAL ENTRY # 2

These past nights I've **<u>SEEN</u>** the CORRUPTION of

the City. It WAS once so beautiful NOW her beauty

is superFICIAL___ … there is ugly CANCER inside

of her. I'll clean out the CANCER CELLS… from

the violent drunks that PUKE on me in the subways

& buses to the diseased WHORES of 42nd street___

I'm SAVING all of them sending them to a Better

Place—And when I'm done with NEW YORK I'll

work my way across the COUNTRY ALL will be

clean & PURE agaiN. I SWEAR IT.

DEMONS

And CHALk outlinE

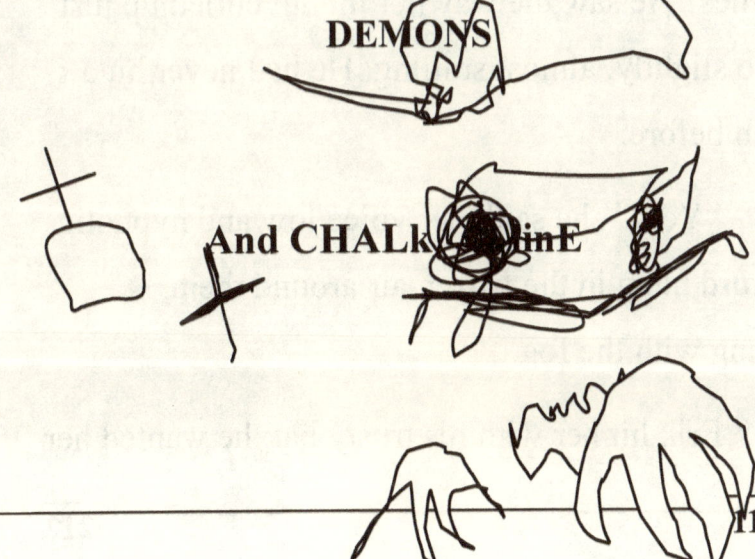

People....

This one was interesting… he could smell the blood on her, even caught an image, but she blocked him somehow. He watched her petite figure, how gracefully and catlike she moved…. Stalking. He followed her for a few blocks, and finally called her in an alley.

"Lamia."

She stopped and turned slightly. The sodium glow of the streetlamp above her turned her pale skin and black hair's shine jaundiced and threw her into shadows. Erik caught a glimpse of her large dark eyes, surrounded in black eyeliner—or was it her eyelashes? He saw the way her mouth curled up just ever so slightly, almost smiling. He had never hit a woman before.

"Yes?" she said, her voice low and hypnotic. The word hung in the frozen air around them, mingling with the fog.

Erik hit her with his trusty bat; he wanted her

death over with as quickly and as painlessly as possible. If he didn't, he'd fall in love with her.

"You'd better have a damned good reason for that, you son of a bitch!" Lamia turned to face him, holding her bleeding head with one hand and catching the bat in midswing with the other. Erik stared in horrified dismay. She should have at least been unconscious from the hit, but she was standing there, and still talking somewhat coherently. She pushed her jaw back into place with an audible snap that made Erik flinch.

Briefly her mind opened to him, as if the wound on her head were a hole to her thoughts. He saw a tall man, a terrifying man, with gaping black eye sockets where eyes should have been and a thin cruel mouth that displayed long jagged teeth tearing their way out of blackened gums. The image was replaced by a memory of two men, both dearly loved… and something else. Lamia could also see into people, and she killed those that deserved it. She was more like him than he had at first realized. He had assumed she was just another stupid Goth that had gotten lost on the way back from the clubs, thinking she was a vampire and killing people. She was so much more.

And she was pulling the bat away from him. Erik heard the sharp metallic clang as it hit the pavement when she threw it away. Lamia smiled at him, exposing her long, sharp eyeteeth, and began to laugh at him.

"You should have used a wood bat, Erik, at least *then* you could have made a stake."

He backed away from her. He could feel her long unseen nails tearing through his mind. She was someone he should never have bothered. Now she was going to make him pay. Painfully.

"Please don't hurt me," Ordinary Erik whimpered. Erik the Vigilante Psychic was just a damned bully and could go to hell. Ordinary Erik just wanted to go back to watching reruns of '70's shows and feasting on microwave dinners fit for one king.

"I won't hurt you," Lamia told him gently.

She held her arms out and Erik walked into them without another thought or image....

The sun set over the Hudson River and the New Jersey skyline as a shadow climbed out of the basement of a condemned factory. It moved silently and without drawing any notice from the emerging club crowd, sliding through alley after alley until it reached its usual haunting grounds. It didn't have long to wait before a drug dealer came around. The shadow moved behind him.

"Hey, Johnny, kill any kids today?"

John Mason turned around and screamed. Erik smiled, his new elongated eyeteeth glinting in the glow of the streetlamps. He didn't need his baseball bat anymore....

THE END